THE CLIQUE
SUMMER COLLECTION

KRISTEN

CLIQUE novels by Lisi Harrison:

THE CLIQUE
BEST FRIENDS FOR NEVER
REVENGE OF THE WANNABES
INVASION OF THE BOY SNATCHERS
THE PRETTY COMMITTEE STRIKES BACK
DIAL L FOR LOSER
IT'S NOT EASY BEING MEAN
SEALED WITH A DISS
BRATFEST AT TIFFANY'S

THE CLIQUE SUMMER COLLECTION:
MASSIE
DYLAN
ALICIA
KRISTEN
CLAIRE (Coming August 5)

THE CLIQUE
SUMMER COLLECTION

KRISTEN

A CLIQUE NOVEL BY
LISI HARRISON

poppy

LITTLE, BROWN AND COMPANY
New York   Boston

Poppy

Little, Brown and Company
Hachette Book Group USA
237 Park Avenue, New York, NY 10017
For more of your favorite series, go to www.pickapoppy.com

First Edition: July 2008

The Poppy name and logo are trademarks of Hachette Book Group USA.

Cover design by Andrea C. Uva
Cover and author photos by Roger Moenks

alloyentertainment
Produced by Alloy Entertainment
151 West 26th Street, New York, NY 10001

ISBN: 978-0-316-02752-6

10 9 8 7 6 5 4 3 2 1
CWO
Printed in the United States of America

For you

"Rate me."

"No."

"Come on, Ms. Gregory. Rate meeee."

"No."

"Kris-*ten*! Come on, pleeeease. You always rate Massie."

"That's different!"

"Just say a number."

"Fine. *Nine*."

"Ehmagawd! I'm a nine!" Ripple Baxter hugged the shell-framed mirror on the living room wall of her father's sea-inspired Westchester summer rental. "I knew this pink snakeskin headband was a must." She petted her deep-fried blond hair.

"Correction." Kristen Gregory sat on the wood-plank floor, then placed her over-sweetened lemonade on the nicked surfboard coffee table. "It's not your score. It's your *age*. You're *nine*. You have to be twelve or older to qualify for a rating." Kristen leered at Ripple from across the musty furnished-by-garage-sale cottage. "Speaking of nine, did you know it's the square root of eighty-one?"

Ignoring her, Ripple turned sideways and examined her

new outfit. A long, pale pink hoodie, meant to cover the hips, practically swallowed the top two thirds of her short, muscular frame. Her knees could have easily been mistaken for extremely saggy boobs, had her purple rhinestone–covered flip-flops not been so close.

"Ripple, your dad is paying me to teach you math and if you don't—"

"Ms. Gregory, he does not, not, *not* care about *math*." Ripple fluffed the dark lashes around her light brown eyes. "All he cares about are waves. He just wants someone to look after me so he can drive out to Long Island and surf. You're more like a tutor-sitter. Heavy on the 'sitter.'"

Funny. Lately Kristen felt *heavy* on everything. How could she not? While she was sweating in a six-week summer school program, Massie was in Southampton, Alicia was in Spain, and Dylan was in Hawaii. Even Claire had left town. True, she'd gone back to Orland-*ew*, but it was better than tutor-sitting a bratty nine-year-old for eighth-grade wardrobe money. When would it be *her* turn to make memories? And when would Ripple stop calling her—

"Ms. Gregory!" Ripple flipped up her pink hood and checked her reflection in the mirror again. "The only thing you can teach me is how to *be* Massie Block."

"You could start by lowering that hood," Kristen blurted, then immediately hate-pinched her own leg for encouraging the little wannabe.

Ripple did as she was told, then reached into her Coach

Heritage Stripe Swingpack knockoff and pulled out ten plastic purple bangles. Glued around them was a white price tag that said 5 FOR $2. "Left or right?" She lifted her wrists. "WWMD?"

Kristen stood and shuffled across the uneven wood floor in Steve Madden cork wedges, her pleated Diesel denim mini swaying below her tight yellow Lacoste halter. "Massie wouldn't do *either*!" She grabbed Ripple's soon-to-be-bangled wrists and pulled her back to the coffee table. "They're *H&M*!"

"Well, then, what *would* she do?" Ripple widened her light brown eyes in anticipation and propped her elbows on the surfboard table.

Kristen squeezed the gold Coach locket Massie had sent her for her birthday—complete with a group photo of the Pretty Committee inside—and thought, *What* would *Massie do?* But not being an alpha, Kristen wasn't completely sure.

"She would do her homework, *okay*?" Kristen lied, flipping open Ripple's crisp, unused math textbook. "Now, if a carton of eggs was one-fifty yesterday and is fifty percent off today, how much are the eggs? A, a dollar; B, two twenty-five; or C, seventy-five cents?"

Ripple plopped down on the green and blue Hawaiian print–covered futon, annoyed. "Why won't you *help* me?"

"Because it's illegal to help a stalker." Kristen ran her hand along her stubbly calf, thinking that the best part of her pathetic day might be the leg-shave bath she had scheduled before bed.

"I am not, not, *not* a stalker!" Ripple whipped the purple bangles across the room. They bounced twice before settling into a cheap plastic heap.

"Then focus and answer the question!" Kristen shouted, grateful that they were the only ones home.

"Wait, I have a better question." Ripple sniffled. "If your three-week crush told you surf chicks were 'cute 'n' all'"— she air-quoted—"but that some sophisticated older girl named Massie Block was super hot, what would *you* do?" She stood and paced. "Would you A, want to figure out the price of eggs; B, stay true to your surfer roots; or C, ask your dad to hire you the summer math tutor who just happens to be Massie's BFF?"

Kristen's stomach lurched. "You're using me for Massie info?"

Ripple smeared glittery pink drugstore gloss on her droopy bottom lip. "It's not using if you're paying."

Kristen felt dizzy. In that very instant, her entire world had just been turned upside down and dumped like a giant handbag. Yes, she was getting paid, but that was supposed to be for her alpha mind, nawt her alpha friend. So what made *her* special now? Once again, being Massie's BFF was her only claim to fame. Her intelligence was meaningless. *Gawd!* If the game Rock, Paper, Scissors were real life, it would be called Brains, Beauty, Brawn. And Beauty would beat Brains and Brawn every time.

Someone kicked the front door open. "Hello? Anyone

home?" A thick beam of sunlight seeped inside the dark cabin. There stood a shirtless boy. It was as if he'd been summoned by God and delivered by angels.

"Dune?" Ripple ran to greet her brother. "What're ya doin' home?"

The thirteen-year-old surf star dropped his salty backpack and took off his white straw fedora. Blond hair the color of Baked Lays swung above his shoulders as he lovingly hugged his sister back.

Awwww.

"Coach kicked me off the team." He shrugged like someone who cared but didn't want anyone to know.

"Why?"

"Last night, the Atlantic was all lit up with phosphorescence. It was past curfew, but I had to paddle out and—"

"In the *dark*?" Ripple gasped, finally sounding like a nine-year-old.

"It was totally worth it." He rubbed his bare chest. "I caught a six-foot left and the water was glowing all green and everyone came out to watch and—" He stepped down the single step that led to the sunken living room and plucked a plastic McIntosh from a bowl of fake fruit on the rickety end table. "Who's this?" He tossed the red apple in the air and caught it.

Kristen's skin stung the way it had when Principal Burns announced, to the entire school, that she had been named captain of the soccer team. He looked right at her, and she blushed as though there were a hundred of him.

"Hey, I'm—"

"Oh, this is Ms. Gregory, my tutor." Ripple flirt-knocked the apple out of Dune's hand and giggled when it rolled across the floor.

"Stop calling me that!" Kristen reddened again, this time from rage. She was nawt going to be used and humiliated by a *nine*-year-old. As soon as their father came home, she was going to quit. Westchester was packed with mathtards. She'd find someone new to tutor by sundown—someone with air-conditioning and decent snacks.

"Hey." He snicker-waved, unsure what to call her. "I'm Dune."

Kristen remembered seeing him at Briarwood's wave pool dedication ceremony last spring, but she'd been so distracted by her then-crush Griffin Hastings, she hadn't noticed what a perfect hang-ten Dune was.

Ehmagawd! Kristen swallowed hard. Did she actually just think that? Whenever she had super-cheesy thoughts like "a perfect hang-ten," she was entering crush mode. "You can call me—"

"Ripple!" Dune suddenly noticed his sister's pink headband, matching sweatshirt, and purple rhinestone flip-flops. "What are you getting tutored in? Looking like an OCDiva?"

Kristen gasped silently. Was that what the surf guys called the girls from Octavian Country Day School.

"Trying," Ripple admitted shamelessly. "And please, from now on, call me Rassie. Like *Massie*, but with an *R*."

Dune hiked up his slouching gold and brown board shorts. "It makes more sense if you lose the *R*."

Ripple whipped a stuffed starfish at his defined shoulders. For the first time in her life, Kristen envied a beige pillow.

"New York sucks." Dune tugged at the shark tooth necklace hanging around his neck, his mood shifting faster than the tides. "I can't believe I'm gonna be landlocked in Westchester all summer."

Just then a large, fit older man padded through the open door, his bare, callused feet slapping against the dark floors like tap shoes. He clapped Dune on the shoulder. "Whose fault is that, son?"

"Dad!" Their shirtless chests slapped as they came together for a hug.

Brice Baxter smiled and ruffled his son's long straight hair. He wore camouflage trunks and a faded yellow DON'T WORRY BE HAPPY baseball cap. "Now go grab your boards. We're going barge surfing."

"But I just styled my hair!" Ripple whined, petting her scalp.

Her father chuckled, never suspecting that his tomboy daughter could have been serious.

"So you're not mad I'm back?" Dune said to the fallen apple on the floor. "Because I sure am."

"Nah." Brice pulled his cap lower. "Your mother will be mad. But that's why we got divorced. That woman cannot go with the flow. I would have been mad if you passed up phosphorescent surf. Besides, the Tavarua trip is coming up. Enjoy the break while you can."

"I guess." Dune's sad brown eyes beamed respect and love for his father.

"You surf, Kristen?" Brice asked, the crispy corners of his hazel eyes scrunching with genuine hospitality. "Because I've been teaching for eighteen years, and I can have you standing by—"

"Um, no. I'm more of a soccer person," she blurted, making it perfectly clear that she was far from an OCDiva.

"Then tell your parents you won't be home for dinner." He rested his arm on her sunburned shoulder. "The Baxters are gonna teach you how to surf."

Without hesitation, Kristen texted her parents, then followed the Baxters out to their blue Chevy Avalanche. Maybe she could give her job one more chance . . . for poor Ripple, of course.

"Okay, kiddos, see that barge over there?" Brice called from the helm of *Old Man*, his buddy's twelve-foot floater. He pointed to the east, the top of his tanned shoulder creasing like a worn leather flat.

Kristen lifted the brim on her moss green and white Chanel bucket hat and searched the middle of the Long Island Sound. Could the floating garbage truck three hundred meters away *possibly* be the barge he was referring to? Even its slow-churning wake looked stinky.

She quickly added a third coat of Clarins SPF 30. The first two were to protect her fair skin from the sun's harmful rays. The last one was to keep the poll-*ew*-tion out.

"Once that baby's close enough, you kids can ride her waves all the way back to Westchester."

"Aiyyyyyyyyyyeeeeeeee!" Dune yelled, tying his blond hair back with a putty-colored rubber band.

"I told you, I am not, not, *not* going in there!" Ripple cried, dumping three bottles of O.P.I. nail polish out of her peach Wet Seal tote and onto her blue striped towel. "Massie would never touch the same water as a gah-ross rat-raft . . . *would* she?" Her wide eyes filled with hope as they met Kristen's, as if praying for Massie to have a secret love of barge surfing or a fondness for wading in estuaries.

Puh-lease!

Kristen delighted in shaking her head no.

Ripple gazed out at the navy blue water and sighed. "Didn't think so."

"Suit yourself," Dune said, waxing his pomegranate red Channel Islands surfboard. "Catch!" He threw a faded black wet suit to Kristen. "I hope it's to your liking," he added with a smirk, nodding at the CC logo on her hat and the alligator on her yellow halter, as if mocking and daring her at the same time.

Ehmagawd! Kristen wanted to shout. *I ne-ver buy Chanel. I can't afford it. Massie gave me this hat because she said my straw Club Monaco was more like a Club Monac-oh-no-you-dizn't. And I have to wear something on my head or I'll get fried. And this halter isn't even real! I bought a pudding-stained Lacoste polo at the Salvation Army, unstitched the alligator, and sewed it on this J. Crew tank. I do that all the time!!! I'm really poor and down-to-earth, like you.*

But instead she caught the stiff black jumper and tried not to gag on the salty rubber smell.

"Thanks." She smiled proudly, hoping he'd noticed her stellar hand-eye coordination.

His wink showed that he had.

All Kristen could do to hide her blushing cheeks and

silence her pounding heart was hurry behind the flapping sails and squeeze into the tight neoprene casing.

"You guys are so *un*," Ripple sighed from her towel. She slid a pair of blush pink knockoff Diors over her heavily shadowed eyes and leaned back on her elbows.

"*Un*-what?" Dune stood over his sister, intentionally casting a buff shadow over her ivory linen–covered body.

"*Un*–everything that's cool." Ripple sat up and jammed a blue foam toe separator between her jagged toenails, then shook a bottle of coral polish.

Dune gave his father a mischievous smile. Brice nodded once, then quickly dropped the anchor into the water with a plop. He raced toward his daughter and, without a single word, grabbed Ripple's legs while Dune gripped her underarms.

"What are you doooooo—"

They carried her toward the edge of the boat while she kicked and flailed like a hooked fish.

"Noooooooo," she pleaded. "I just got this beach cover-up!"

Kristen covered her open mouth—hiding her amusement from Ripple and her shock from Dune.

They swung her once and her glasses fell overboard. Twice and her hair band was gone. The third time they let her go.

"Ahhhhhhh!" Ripple sailed over the rope railings, her blue foam toe separators still intact.

Brice high-fived his son while Kristen finished zipping up

her wet suit and hurried to the boat's edge, careful not to get too close to them, just in case she was next.

"Ehmagawd! It's subarctical." Ripple chattered, wiping her soggy hair away from her shadow-smudged eyes, her linen dress ballooning around her like a white chocolate Hershey's Kiss. "You toe-dally ruined my makeover!"

"That was the point, *Rassie*." Dune got down on his knees and offered her his hand. Ripple grabbed on. But then he immediately let go. "No OCDivas allowed."

Kristen's cheeks burned with shame as Ripple fell back into the muddy water.

"Dune!" Brice snicker-scolded.

"What about *her*?" Ripple grunted as she lifted herself back onto the bobbing boat. "She's a *total* OCDi—"

Uh-oh.

"Last one in pees in their wet suit!" Kristen whipped off her hat and made a running dive off the boat, plunging head-first into the chilly sound. The instant brain freeze sobered her senses, numbing her crush symptoms and returning her to her usual state of controlled fabulousness.

"Whoooooooo-hooooooooo!" Dune ran straight off the boat with his board tucked under his arm. His wet suit remained behind, lying flat on the deck like the chalk outline of a dead body.

"Aren't you freezing?" Kristen asked when he surfaced. She could already feel the sun nibbling at her unprotected cheeks but refused to get out now. Instead, she sliced her legs beneath her, treading water and doing her best not to swallow the murky water.

"Nah." He sat on his surfboard and whipped his head back, slapping his long wet hair against his glistening shoulders.

He smacked his board, inviting Kristen to join him. She glided over, lifted herself up, and in one smooth motion straddle-sat behind him. Unsure of what to do with her hands, she slipped them under her neoprene-covered butt, which felt like a cold seal.

Dune flipped around and faced her. "You might want to take that off."

"What?" Kristen squeaked. She was excited times ten that her crush was obviously crushing back, but come *awn!* Taking things off was moving a little fast, even for a pro surfer. She squint-glanced back up at the boat, wondering if Brice could hear his son's advances. But he was ten feet away, eating a jelly donut and flipping though a copy of *Surfer's Journal,* totally unaware.

"Your *necklace.*" He wrinkled his sunburned nose disapprovingly. "It could break."

Kristen gripped the gold heart-shaped locket around her neck. "Oh." She smile-sighed with relief, while flipping the Coach logo to the back. "I can't. It was a gift from Massie. I pinky-swore I'd keep it on all summer."

"Massie?" Dune narrowed his light brown eyes. "The same Massie who turned my used-to-be-cool sister into a

deck dork?" He chin-pointed at Ripple, who was sitting on her blue-and-white–striped towel trying to rub suntan oil on her lower back. She looked like an angry ape swatting at a mosquito.

Ooops.

Kristen ran her pale fingers through the dark, lapping water to avoid his disapproving gaze. He booger-flicked a piece of sea grass off his board. "A promise is a promise."

"I like that." Dune pinched the shark tooth strung around his neck on what looked like the thick leather lace of an old Topsider. "I made this at surf camp in Cali when I was ten, with my best buddy, Reid. I've never taken it off."

Awwww. Kristen touched her rubber-covered heart. If there was something higher than a hang-ten, he was it. Cute, loyal, athletic, and middle class. Dune was a total CLAM.

"Just make sure it's on tight." He winked and then gazed beyond her shoulder toward the barge.

Afraid of losing his attention to a passing bird or sailboat, Kristen quickly lured him back. "Why do you like surfing so much?" she asked, knowing he would spend hours on the topic if she'd let him.

Dune returned, his eyes darting across her wet cheeks like he was reading her freckles. "For me . . ." He paused thoughtfully. "Surfing is about truth. It's pure. When you're faced with a wave, you can't pretend to be something you're not. Either you can ride it or you can't. There's no faking. It's honest."

Kristen's lips twitched. Her belly bubbled. And the Long Island Sound blurred like it was coated in Vaseline Lip Therapy. Kristen's central nervous system was sending an urgent message: Dune had just received an upgrade. Infatuation just got bumped up to luh-uv. This was serious.

"Look!" he shout-pointed at the barge as it carved through the blue water and tooted toward them.

Kristen began searching her mind for ways to stay in Dune's good graces without risking her life—and pride—riding the wave of a floating garbage truck. But all that came to mind was how much his skin was the color of caramel. And how much she loved caramel.

The barge turned left and began carving out the first set.

"Last one standing has to paint Ripple's toenails!" Brice shouted, leaping up from his perch on *Old Man*. He tossed his burnt orange longboard over the rope rails, then stride-jumped in behind it, landing a couple inches from Kristen and Dune.

"Can you keep treading?" Dune practically shoved Kristen off the board before she had time to answer. He lay flat on his belly and began butterflying his arms toward the swell. "First watch how I do it," he called over the hum of the barge. "Then I'll be back to teach you."

Suddenly, something squirmed inside Kristen's stomach. She ran her hand along the belly of her wet suit, wondering if maybe a sea creature had wiggled its way inside. But there was nothing there. Just the sickening feeling of abandonment.

What now? Her heart began to thump like the techno beat in the Spanish pop songs Alicia kept e-mailing the Pretty Committee. There she was in the middle of the Long Island Sound without a board, a crush, or a clue.

Thankfully, the water remained relatively flat. In fact, Dylan could fart bigger waves in the Blocks' Jacuzzi. Maybe they got bigger as they got closer? Kristen took a few strokes toward Dune and Brice, hoping for some insight.

TOOOOOOOOOOOOOOOT.

"Dad, are you serious?" Dune asked as his father paddled up beside him. His board barely bobbed as the first set passed underneath. "It's completely dead out here."

"SUCKER PUNCH!" Brice shouted. He stopped paddling, leaned over, and playfully cuffed his son on the back of his leg. "I can't believe you fell for *barge* surfing."

Dune's mouth hung open, somewhere between embarrassment and amusement. "I can't believe you lied to me!"

"It got your mind off the tour, didn't it?" he chuckled.

Dune slowly turned and glanced back at Kristen. "Yeah, I guess." He smiled. The sun kissed his full lips, and the warm breeze blew it straight to her cheek.

She lifted her face to the cloudless sky and grinned peacefully, as if treading water in the Long Island Sound was the new yoga. It didn't matter that Kristen had been the first one in the water—she still peed her wet suit.

Ahhhhhhhh.

Kristen pressed a cold can of Diet Coke against her sun-fried cheeks, even though her left knee was burning up. It had been pressed against Dune's leg for the entire drive back to Westchester and was IM'ing severe crush warnings to every other part of her body.

"Dad! Stop the truck!" Dune slapped his hand against the Chevy's back window and unsnapped his seat belt. "Drop me here." He pulled his knee away and Kristen instantly lost her heat, like an unplugged flatiron.

The sprawling green grounds of the Westchester Country Club were just ahead. As always, the majestic stone clubhouse seemed to glare at her with condescension, reminding Kristen that even though she had eaten in the Blocks' formal dining room with Massie—twice—she definitely did not belong.

It was shocking that Dune wanted to stop within a mile of the ultra-exclusive club. From what Kristen knew, it seemed like the kind of place that would make his down-to-earth CLAM blood boil. But as the truck slowed to a stop, it all became clear—the grinding sound of wheels zipping across the pavement, the clusters of helmet-wearing kids addicted to Red Bull and bruises, the rolling asphalt hills. They had arrived at Gray Acres Skate Park, or GAS Park as it was fondly called.

"Anyone else coming?" Dune grabbed his yellow, purple, and green striped Element skateboard out from under his seat, opened the car door, and jumped onto the sidewalk. He balanced his board on the curb like a seesaw and then popped an ollie.

"Not, not, *not* a chance," Ripple muttered, flipping through the pages of *Teen Vogue*. She drew a lopsided heart around a turquoise pair of Diane von Furstenberg shorts she'd never be able to afford.

"Why not?" Kristen asked, surveying the crowd. All the super-size clothing and Billabong hats made it impossible to tell whether they were girls or boys.

"I can't, Ms. Gregory! Look at me!" Ripple screeched at her reflection in the rearview mirror and then turned to her brother. "My hair is all frizzy and my makeup washed off, thanks to *you* and *Dad*," she practically spat.

"Who cares, Rassie?" Dune joked, kick-flipping the board off the ground and into his hand.

"Since when do you care what you look like at the GAS?" Brice turned around to face his daughter. It was the first time his expression had been somewhat serious. Now that his face was relaxed, thin white lines of untanned skin were suddenly visible at the corners of his eyes—proving that whenever Brice was in the sun, he was smiling.

"Um, did you ever happen to notice the country club on the other side of the fence?" Ripple slid down on the tan leather interior to avoid being spotted.

"Unfortunately, yes, but I never thought you did." Dune shook his head in disgust. "Jeez, Rassie. If you ever run into my *cool* sister, Ripple, tell her I say hi. I'm outie like a belly button."

"Who cares? I still have math homework. Right, Ms. G?"

"Nope." Kristen placed her hand on Ripple's muscular, damp linen–covered shoulder. "We're done for the day." She added pressure, hoping her student would get the hint.

"Baxter?" a white-blond boy called loudly from the top of the half-pipe.

"Heyyyyy!" Dune tucked his skateboard under his arm and jogged away.

"Buzz me if you need a ride home," Brice called after him.

Dune signaled "okay" with a backhanded wave just as Ripple turned down the corner of a page showing a gold Juicy charm bracelet.

"Let's *go*!" Kristen insisted to Ripple through gritted teeth.

Ripple snapped her head up from the magazine. "Why? Is Massie into skating?" Once again her light brown eyes filled with hope.

"She's got a board in her closet." Kristen tugged her arm. "Now come awn!"

"*Really?*"

"Yup. Really." It happened to be an emery board, but why get technical?

"Then let's go, go, go!" Ripple crawled over her tutor-sitter and jumped onto the curb. "Bye, Dad! We'll call when we're done."

Just before slamming the door shut, Kristen took off her green Chanel logo bucket hat and tossed it onto the seat. Dune's disapproving glare had burned her more than the sun's rays. And its effects were more lasting too.

"You're not wearing it?"

Before Kristen could answer, Ripple scooped the hat off the seat and forced it over her fried blond hair.

With renewed confidence, she led the way around a drained three-leaf clover pool, past the mini jungle gym in the kiddie section, and straight to the half-pipe, where Dune was knuckle-bashing his buddies. Along the way, they passed clusters of skinny, wool cap–wearing boys. Ripple lifted her long horse nose a little higher each time one of them waved hello.

"You *know* all these guys?" Kristen asked, feeling some-what impressed by her otherwise unimpressive student.

"I used to skate with them," Ripple muttered, lifting her nose once again. Kristen could see straight into her nostrils. "But that was before I . . ." She paused as they reached

Dune and his friends—three boys whose bare chests peeked out over varying shades of skinny jeans.

"Whad'up, Rip?" A thin blonde with narrow green eyes, a light smattering of freckles, and a black arm cast lifted his free palm.

Ripple waved away his attempted high five as if it had been double-dipped in puke. "Ew, Tyler, there's, like, dirt on your hand."

He took a close look, shrugged, and then licked it clean.

"Gah-rosss!" Ripple screeched, covering her eyes with *Teen Vogue*. Kristen crinkled her sunburned nose in disgust, just like Massie would have done.

But Dune and the other boys burst out laughing. And while it was tempting to join in the hysterics because his response *was* funny, it was too late. She had already nose-crinkled. And there was no coming back from that.

"Kristen." Dune reached out and pulled her deeper into their circle. "These are my boys, Tyler, Jax, and Scooter."

"Hey." Kristen beamed, having no idea who was who and not caring one bit. How could she? Dune had touched her . . . in public . . . in front of his friends. There wasn't enough room in her brain for anything other than those three things to register.

They greeted her with lifted hands. Then, without another word, the one with the curly blond hair and bulging blue eyes—Scooter?—slammed down his board, pushed off, and teetered onto the half-pipe. His wheels rumbled each time he rose and fell in the giant plywood smile. Kristen wondered how long it would be before Dune left to join him. The thought of losing him made her stomach dip like she was the one skating down the U.

"Hey, Rip, where'dya get that lid?" asked the guy she'd decided must be Jax, a boy with limp brown hair that covered his dark eyes. It hung like the sleepy branches of the weeping willow on the other side of the tall wood fence—the country club side.

Ripple swayed from side to side like a shy little girl. "Paris," she lied, avoiding Kristen's eyes.

"Paris *Hilton*, maybe!" Jax blurted. "SUCKER PUNCH!" He leaned over and knocked Ripple on the side of her arm.

"Ow-*ie*." She rubbed it like it hurt, but blushed like she enjoyed it.

"Oooof!" Scooter grunted from the half-pipe. "My coccyx!" He lay splayed on the bottom of the half-pipe, grabbing his bum, completely oblivious to the other riders zipping by.

"Get up before someone grinds you into a smoothie!" Jax called.

Tyler and Dune snickered. Their camaraderie made Kristen long for the familiarity of the Pretty Committee, but at the same time, she was thankful they were miles away. If they knew she was hanging at GAS—voluntarily—she'd be teased more than Amy Winehouse's hair. According to them, her world was on the other side of the fence . . . or at least, it used to be. Now she had no idea what side she belonged on—the one she could afford, or the one she *wanted* to afford? Before she'd met Dune, that answer had been easy.

"So, do you guys go to Briarwood?" Kristen blurted, showing Dune she would become buds with his friends. She'd never be the kind of girl who would make him choose.

At first no one responded. They were too busy laughing at Scooter, who was now on all fours struggling to stand. Except Ripple. She was busy fussing with the Chanel cap, turning the logo to face the back.

Jax finally spoke up. "We're at Abner Double Day. Us ADD boys aren't good enough for those fancy private schools." He middle-parted his long brown hair into an upside-down V—it looked like he was peeking through tent flaps.

"Oh, I only go to one because I'm on scholarship." Kristen rolled her eyes, like attending OCD was more embarrassing than period-stained jeans. She quickly turned to Tyler. "So, what's with the cast?"

Tyler lifted his elbow and checked his arm like he had just noticed it was covered in black plaster.

"Incoming!" Out of nowhere, Jax shoved Tyler, Kristen, Dune, and Ripple three feet to the left as a white golf ball careened through the blue sky. It landed with a thud on the beige wood beside them, then rolled down into the half-pipe.

"Fire in the hole!" shouted a green-haired skater, who managed to turn his deck seconds before the speeding orb would have lodged under his wheels and sent him flying.

The rest of the riders jumped off their boards and knee-slid to the flat part of the pipe.

"Learn how to hit a ball, Nantucket Red!" yelled someone wearing a red helmet covered in cartoon rats.

When the ball finally settled on the plywood, Scooter grabbed it, covered his left nostril, and blew hard through his right. Once the ball was fully covered in snot, he whipped it back over the fence with a grunt.

Everyone at the park applauded, except for Kristen, whose hands were being used to block her mouth from projectiling. And Ripple. She'd laced her fingers behind her back when she realized Massie's BFF found the whole display nauseating times ten.

"*That's* what happened," Tyler spat. "Freaking CC, man. I rode over one of their balls and ate it."

Dune immediately burst out laughing. At first Tyler looked at him in confusion but then something clearly clicked inside his mind and he began cracking up. The part of Kristen that belonged on the GAS side of the fence wanted to crack up too. But the side of her that had been a guest at the CC told her it was best not to. Unsure of what to do, she let out a half laugh that sounded more like a half sneeze.

"Did you hear what he just said?" Dune slapped Jax on his bare back. But Jax was focusing on a group of preppy girls *ew*-ing at what had just come flying over the fence. He shook his head, sending his hair tent-flapping back over his face. He hopped on his board and dropped into the half-pipe. "Whooooooooo!" he shouted, obviously wanting to be noticed.

"Is he still sweating those OCDivas?" Dune furrowed his tan forehead.

Tyler nodded yes, picking at his cast.

"Why?"

Tyler shook his head like he had no idea.

"How lame," Kristen insisted. "Can't they make a rule? Something that would keep the balls away from GAS?"

They all burst out laughing again, except Ripple, who was now checking her gloss in a black Sephora compact—the one that came free with a purchase of Jessica Simpson's body cream.

"The country club is pissed that we board so close to their property. They think we're loud and ugly," Tyler answered. "So they started letting the beginners tee off from the fourth green, which is right over there." He pointed over the fence to a group of knock-kneed, madras shorts–wearing wannabes working on their swings.

"Gawd." Kristen crossed her arms over her chest in a gesture that she hoped conveyed disgust and contempt for the rich.

"Tons of skaters have gone down." Dune looked Kristen right in the eye. His commitment to her in that moment made her sunburned cheeks overheat.

"But there's an upside." Tyler grabbed a pack of chocolate-flavored Bubblicious out of his back pocket and popped a piece in his mouth without offering any to his friends. "The trust fund skaters have been scared off, like the Briarwood Academy soccer boys. Now those cleat-feet hang out at Andy Ryan's house, cuz he has a half-pipe."

"And that hot sister, Olivia," Jax added, suddenly appearing behind them.

"Olivia's not, not, not *that* pretty," Ripple pout-mumbled.

And there's nothing wrong with cleat-feet! Kristen wanted to shout. But she decided to save her outbursts for later— when she and Dune were a couple and she didn't have to worry about impressing his friends.

"Hey, got any more gum?" Jax held out his dirty palm.

Tyler dug around the inside of his pocket and pulled out the pack. Jax, Dune, and Ripple all grabbed pieces. Kristen extended her arm, but Tyler casually pulled the pack away, leaving her to chew on the bitter taste of not being accepted.

"Sorry, dude, I never give the last piece."

"Since when?" Dune flicked his buddy's black cast.

Tyler snicker-shrugged.

"You can share mine, Ms. Gregory," Ripple said as she attacked the brown cube with her slightly buck teeth.

"It's okay," Kristen managed.

Dune's eyes lingered on her, searching for clues to the contrary. But life with the rich and fabulous Pretty Committee had taught Kristen to hide her feelings of inadequacy by batting her lashes and smiling brightly. Her tears got the hint to come back when she was alone.

"Anyhow, we have to get back at the CC." Jax ran a hand through his sweaty bangs. "I say we drain their pool and skate it."

"And when we're done, let's fill it back up with Jell-O," Dune added. "Some guy on YouTube did it to his uptight neighbor. It was a total sucker punch!"

Jax spit his gum into his hand, then whipped it over the fence. "Dude, that's way too hard."

Ripple giggled. "I love how you just threw that."

Jax shot her a polite half smile, then wiped his goober-filled hand on the side of his jeans.

"What about filling it with golf balls?" Tyler tried.

"Dumb." Dune flicked his cast again.

"Stop doing that!" Tyler snicker-shoved Dune into Scooter, who had just returned from his skate to rejoin the circle, still perched by the lip of the half-pipe.

"Shhh! Country Club Chick is coming over!" Jax shoved all three of them.

"Her?" Ripple scoffed as if they were talking about Ugly Betty. "You like *her*? She's, like, *obsessed* with dancing. It's totally weird."

Kristen turned to see who it was and gasped. "Ehma-gawd!"

Super-blond, super-tanned, super-flexible Skye Hamilton, the infamous eighth-grade alpha, was scurrying over the fence wearing nothing but a yellow string bikini and a glittery orange scarf. She jumped down onto the asphalt like the bottoms of her bare feet were coated in Nike rubber. "Heyyy, yooouuuuuuu!" She tossed her curly hair and waved her flawlessly manicured Nars Pleasantly Pink nails as she approached.

Her blond besties (known as the DSL Daters because they made super-fast connections with boys) gripped the metal links from the country club side like inmates hungry for a glimpse of the outside world.

Scooter swallowed nervously, then turned and dropped back into the half-pipe.

"Hey." Tyler awkwardly lifted his cast to wave.

"Hey." Jax shook his head until his bangs grazed the top of his nose.

Ripple rolled her eyes.

Skye smiled sweetly at everyone but came to a complete stop in front of Dune.

"Hey, hey, whaddaya say?" She pliéd twice, then stood. "I thought you were gonna be gone all summer?"

"Just got back." Dune smiled.

Kristen's eyes searched his face for clarification. Was it the I'm-just-being-polite smile? Or the let's-lip-kiss smile? It was hard to tell.

"What are you hotties doing tomorrow?" Skye twirled a deep-conditioned golden lock around her finger, sending a heap of gold bangles jangling down her arm.

"Nuthin'." Jax's voice cracked a little.

Ripple rolled her eyes again.

"Perf!" She turned and flashed a thumbs-up to her friends, who bounced up and down on their toes and air-clapped. "Then I'll put your names on the list at the club. We'll hang by the pool. See ya around elevenish?"

"We're in!" Jax blurted, this time in a faux-deep voice.

"Killer bees!" Skye hop-turned into a glissée tour jeté and darted back to the fence. Heads turned like searchlights as she passed.

"You guys are not, not, *not* really going, are you?" Ripple's light brown eyes darted from one boy's face to the next. But they all had the same dumbstruck expression—like they had each discovered hundred-dollar bills in their pockets.

"Yeah, we are." Jax grinned.

"Sellout!" Tyler lifted his cast, reminding them that she was the enemy.

"She's lame anyway," Kristen finally chimed in. "She totally knows me and didn't even say hi! I wouldn't go if I were you. She's not a good friend." Aware that Dune was a stick-up-for-your-buddy kind of guy, Kristen hoped this news would turn him off the dancer for life.

"We have to." Dune gathered his blond hair into a ponytail. "How else are we going to get close to their pool?"

"Or their . . ." Jax gripped invisible melons.

The boys burst out laughing. Ripple sighed like a frustrated parent and stormed off.

"Is that what this is really about?" Tyler pressed. "A pool prank?"

"Yeah. What else would it be?" Dune insisted, the sides of his mouth straining to hold back a betraying smile.

"You tell me." Tyler folded his arms across his bare chest.

Kristen waited along with everyone else for him to answer. Her heart thumped louder and louder with every passing millisecond that he stood and contemplated. Suddenly, he leaped forward, grabbed Tyler's board out of his good hand, and rode it onto the half-pipe. "SUCKER PUNCH!" he shouted as he rolled away.

It was far from the reaction Kristen had been hoping for, but it wasn't the one she'd feared either. Once again she was unsure of where she stood. And once again she would have to straddle both sides until she could figure it out.

Kristen woke up in her white Pottery Barn twin bed spooning David Beckham. Her top arm rose and fell with his breath, a gentle rhythm like the lazy sway of a hammock. It had offered her solace many times in the past. Like the time she'd gotten a super-short boy cut. Or when she'd gotten kicked out of OCD. And even a few weeks ago, after her parents had announced she'd be spending another boring summer at home. But this morning, no matter how hard she side-hugged her fluffy white Persian kitty, Kristen could not get rid of the churn in her stomach. In fact, every time she thought about her visit to GAS Park it got bigger. But why? Was it:

A) Her inability to be instantly adored by Dune's friends?

B) Dune's failure to hint at follow-up plans when they'd parted ways?

C) Skye Hamilton's Dune-or-die attitude?

D) Skye Hamilton and her good-luck-competing-with-my-hotness confidence?

E) Knowing that Dune would be at the country club

in less than two hours flirting with Skye Hamilton and the DSL Daters?

F) Not having any plans on her day off?

G) All of the above. ✓

The answer was clear. It was G, all of the above. And choosing G meant texting M, aysap.

Kristen lifted her arm off David Beckham and palm-patted her night table. She knuckle-bumped her hard copy of *The Daring Book for Girls*, an empty bottle of Vitamin Water, the base of her lime-green lamp, which matched the painted walls perfectly, and finally, her black Razr. Sitting up, she pulled David Beckham onto her lap, pushed back the sleeves of her A&F periwinkle blue sleep shirt, and flipped open her phone. Her thumbs took care of the rest.

K: crush x 10 on Dune Baxter. Skye 2. How do I win?

Kristen dragged her gold locket from one side of the chain to the other while she waited for a response. Did she sound too desperate? Too insecure? Too—

Ping.

M: Dune the SURFER?

K: Y!

Ping.

M: Is he endorsed?
K: N.

Ping.

M: Rich parents?
K: N.

Ping.

M: Then Dune's done.

Ping.

M: Dune = D-EW-N

Ping.

M: Wave goodbye.

Ping.

M: Get it? ☺

"Ugh!" Kristen snapped her phone shut and self-pity-whipped it across the room. It landed in the middle of her sea blue beanbag with a thud-hiss.

Gawd! How many expensive lattes had she sipped listening to Massie talk about Derrington and Chris Abeley? And how insulting was it to dismiss Dune as a crush candidate just because he was ATM-challenged. Especially knowing Kristen was on scholarship. It was more un*fair* than Dune's deeply tanned skin.

Even if Kristen *wanted* to turn to her mother for advice—which she didn't, because she would be told to avoid boys and stay focused on work and school so she could learn to thrive in this world without a man—she couldn't. Marsha Gregory was at Costco. And her father, Ray, was on a golf trip in Miami working on some potential new business venture. A trip that Marsha swore would be his last as a walking man if he didn't return with a signed contract big enough to get them out of debt after his last "potential new business venture."

There was only one place left to turn.

Kristen closed her bedroom door. Lowered her bamboo shades. Yanked her mother's old yellow dishwashing gloves out from under her mattress and slid them on. Then she crouched beside David Beckham's kitty litter box, dug in, and pulled out Dylan's white hand-me-down MacBook. Tiny powder-scented rocks fell away to the sides and split like Demi Moore's middle part. But the thick Saran Wrap coating kept the secret computer preserved and protected from feline waste. Not that it was necessary. David Beckham was fully potty trained and hadn't used the box for years. Not even when he had had that bladder infection over Easter.

Under the dark cover of her blue and green polka-dot duvet, Kristen powered up the old laptop. It inhaled deeply, then whirred to life like an asthmatic. She unfastened a black code key from the tiny Velcro straps she'd secretly attached on the wall side of her bed. Then she flipped the face of her silver Guess Carousel watch over to its LCD screen side. As soon as the red flashes came, she inserted the code key into the computer's USB port, then held up her wrist.

Beep, beep, beep.

Kristen pulled out the key and breathed a sigh of relief as the watch screen flashed. SIGNAL SENT.

Help was on the way.

Transformation took thirty-four seconds. That was three seconds faster than last time. And it gave Kristen a chance to check her costume in the mirror before *they* arrived.

"Good morning, Cleopatra," she greeted her reflection with a proud smile. It was too bad she couldn't wear the black bob-with-bangs wig in public, because it really brought out the green in her eyes. And the white goddess dress dripping with gold chains showed off her toned shoulders. The creamy blue eye shadow would have looked better had Kristen's cheeks not been bright red from yesterday's sunburn. But the gold headband with the snake emblem pulled attention away from her face and drew it up, toward her royal brain. And *that* was her most important asset. Because Kristen Gregory was the alpha of the ultra-exclusive Witty Committee.

She had founded the secret underground organization last June after her first week of gifted extra-credit summer classes. The Pretty Committee was gone. Soccer was done until September. The *New York Times* crossword puzzle just wasn't challenging anymore. And she was so emotional that repeat episodes of *The Hills* were moving her to tears. She was hovering over that place—right before rock bottom—where she could either rise up and turn her life around or fall flat on her face.

Around the same time, her teacher, Ms. Lobe, asked all five students in the class to write a paper on a gifted person—living or dead—whom they admired most. Kristen had picked the queen of Egypt.

Cleopatra had learned how to speak Egyptian (hard times ten) and was the leader of an empire, the mother of four, and hawt! Not even Angelina Jolie could claim all of that. Her other classmates had picked their favorites, and for the rest of the week they'd had to come to class in costume in order to *be* their alphas. It was the most fun Kristen had ever had. Even more fun than Massie's Friday night sleepover where they'd photographed Bean in eight different bikinis and e-mailed the shots to *Teen Vogue*.

When the exercise had ended and life had returned to normal, a heavy listlessness had weighed on the students like a humid afternoon. Without exchanging a single word or glance with her classmates, Kristen could sense that for them, as for her, a part of them had died.

But without the excuse of "class assignment" or "Halloween costume," no one dared go out in public dressed as their favorite Gifted, unless of course they wanted their house wrapped in Cottonelle by snickering neighborhood kids. And that was nothing compared to what Massie and the Pretty Committee would do to Kristen if they discovered she enjoyed dressing up with LBRs more than shopping with the PC.

So for now, and probably forever, the Witty Committee would be Kristen's biggest secret. Biggest savior. And biggest joy. When they were together, money and looks didn't matter. Brains did. And the only other place on the planet like that was the Genius Bar at the Mac Store. It was *that* rare.

"THE COMMITTEE IS ASSEMBLED," announced the computer-generated voice from the speaker on Dylan's white ex-MacBook.

Kristen hurried away from the mirror, sat on her bed, and propped the computer up on her lap.

The screen was divided into quarters, each quadrant containing one of the members' faces. (Bill Gates's idea, obvs.)

EINSTEIN (Layne Abeley)	**BILL GATES (Danh Bondok)**
Disguise: tweed coat, bushy mustache, wiry gray wig	**Disguise:** glasses, light blue button-down, dark blue blazer
Expertise: physics	**Expertise:** technology
OPRAH (Rachel Walker)	**SHAKESPEARE (Aimee Snyder)**
Disguise: wavy black wig, gold hoop earrings, pumpkin orange blouse	**Disguise:** gray bald-in-the-front, curly-in-the-back wig, mustache, white collar sticking out of a black cloak
Expertise: anthropology (the study of humankind, not the cute and affordable shabby-chic store)	**Expertise:** affairs of the heart and the Romance languages

"Thank you for gathering," Kristen told her betas, starting into the eye of her MacBook. "What do we stand for?"

"BOB," they answered.

"And what does BOB stand for?" Kristen asked.

"Brains over beauty!"

She smile-nodded at each one of them, then proceeded, before they were interrupted and forced to demobilize.

"I'm in crush conflict," she whispered, leaning in toward the screen.

Bill Gates took off his glasses and thumb-rubbed his eyes. Behind him was a poster that read MEGABYTE ME!

"I tutor-sit a surf girl named Ripple who hired me to

teach her math, but only because she wants to know about Massie. I was going to quit, but then I met her brother. And he's a ten."

Danh Bondok/Bill Gates started blinking rapidly. His fluttering black lashes revealed a yearlong crush on Kristen. But inter-committee relationships were forbidden, a rule she'd instated last Valentine's Day after Dahn sent her e-roses and figured out a way to make their sweet smell waft out of her computer.

"He's a surfer/skater who's totally down-to-earth and loyal to his friends."

"Loyalty is an important quality in a mate." Rachel Walker/Oprah grinned peacefully.

"I *know*." Kristen beamed, feeling proud of her boy-choice. "He's anti-OCDiva, which had me scared at first, but I was doing a good job of showing him the *other* me," Kristen's cheeks turned red with shame as she suddenly realized the *other* her was actually the *real* her. "And he was into it, until a blond alpha named Skye Hamilton came along and invited him to hang at the country club. A place he says he *hates*."

"Then *why* did he accept her invitation?" Oprah put her thumb under her chin and leaned forward in anticipation of the answer.

"A chemical we produce called pheromones may be at play here," explained Layne Abeley/Einstein. "He may not be able to control his attraction. It's quite possibly physiological."

Kristen huffed. She didn't want the case closed so quickly and resented Einstein's theory.

"I think he may have a crush on her. But he *claims* he wants to check out the pool for a prank."

They looked confused.

"He wants to drain it, skate it, then fill it back up with Jell-O," Kristen explained, and then wished she could take it back. Her crush was coming off as a tool bag, and she didn't want the Witty Committee to lose respect for her. But if anyone understood fools in love, it would be the girl on the lower right of her screen. "Shakespeare, what should I do? How do I turn this love triangle into a heart?"

Aimee Snyder/Shakespeare cleared her throat and straightened her bald-in-front, curly-in-the-back wig. "Let's start by clarifying the true nature of a love triangle."

Everyone rolled their eyes.

"In *Twelfth Night*, Orsino loves Olivia. Olivia loves Cesario. And Cesario, who is really Violet dressed as a man, loves Orsino. *That's* a triangle. What you're experiencing is more like a love *V*. Dune is the point in the middle. You are on the left, and Skye is on the right." She squint-paused. "Actually, maybe it's a love *W*. He's the spike caught between the two of you."

"Control alt delete!" Bill Gates snapped. "None of this makes sense. Either he likes you or he doesn't. And if he *doesn't*, I suggest you reboot and move on to someone who does."

"Nonsense," Oprah snapped. "The universe will give this to you if it's meant to be. Compromise with Ripple. You teach her what Massie likes *if* she teaches you what Dune likes. Once you understand him better, you'll know if you're true soul mates."

"In the meantime," Einstein chimed in, "Bill Gates and I will try to figure out how to make the Jell-O in the pool work. If you can help him pull that off, he'll probably think you're pretty cool."

"It's a rather uninspired prank if you ask me." Bill removed his glasses and dabbed his forehead with the gray felt usually used to clean computer screens. "But chilling gallons of sugary water in July will be a fun challenge." He put his glasses back on. "And something *he* obviously couldn't manage on his own."

"Honnnn-eyyyy, I'm home!" Marsha Gregory called from across the condo. "Costco was a madhouse and I forgot to bring my own bags."

David Beckham scurried out from under the blue and green polka-dot duvet and Kristen pulled off her wig and stuffed it behind her pillow. "Hi, Mom."

She turned to dismiss the Witty Committee, but they were already gone.

Kristen shimmied her butt up the Baxters' gritty sloping roof and repositioned herself in the center of her nubby coral beach towel. Ripple had suggested they spend their study session elevated so they could be closer to the sun's tanning rays. And in the spirit of Oprah's suggestion to compromise, Kristen had agreed. But her sizzling skin, which now matched her bright red bikini, had a different opinion.

Below, Brice was speed-loading his board on top of the Chevy. He'd just gotten a call that the waves on Fire Island were going off, and he was determined to catch the one-thirty ferry.

Dune was already at the skate park—at least, that was what Ripple had told Kristen. For all she knew he was sipping virgin coladas by the pool with alpha soon-to-be-ninth-grader Skye Hamilton, drawing coconut-scented Hawaiian Tropic hearts on her zitless back.

"Next question," Kristen groaned, trying to stay focused, at least while her employer was still within earshot. "In fourteen hundred ninety-two—"

"Ms. Gregory, I do not, not, *nawt* care about fourteen hundred ninety-two. Massie wasn't even *alive* then." Ripple

43

pursed her Vincent Longo Bronzella—coated lips and rolled over onto her flat belly. The 3-D daisy on the butt of her yellow bikini was flattened, and two of its petals were bent. Her fried hair had been over-brushed, causing her spilt ends to stick out like tiny worms trying to warm themselves after a chilly rainfall. "So unless you have a list of fourteen hundred ninety-two ways to become Massie, or fourteen hundred ninety-two ways to convince a crush that you're as *sophisticated* as Massie, then *thisss*"—she pointed at Kristen, then at herself—"is over."

Down in the driveway Brice shielded his eyes from the sun and looked up. "Be good," he called. Then he waved goodbye and quickly jumped in his truck, like a boy desperate to escape before his mother saddled him with a list of chores.

Once the engine had started and the blue truck was reversing out of the cracked driveway, Kristen snapped the history book shut. "You're totally right." She rolled onto her stomach and turned to Ripple, ignoring the blue textbook as it slid toward the eave. "I was just trying to look professional until your dad left."

"Really?" Ripple raised a blond brow.

"Pinky-swear." Kristen held out her finger.

Ripple practically lunged for it.

"I was thinking. . . ." Kristen summoned Oprah's plan. "The only way for you to truly understand Massie is if we go shopping."

"Seriously?" Ripple beamed.

Kristen smiled back. "Yes."

"No, no, no wayyyyyyyyyyyy!" Ripple rolled onto her back and bicycled her blond hair–covered legs in the air.

"Who knows?" Kristen lowered the brim on the old brown Von Dutch trucker hat she'd found in the back of her closet, something she'd decided to wear BMB (behind Massie's back) in case Dune was home. "Maybe you could put a fourth-grade Itty Bitty Pretty Committee together and be their alpha."

Ripple kicked her legs harder.

"*Iffff* you do one thing for me . . ."

Ripple stopped pedaling and lowered her legs.

"What," she said, like it wasn't a question.

"You teach me how to dress to impress a skater, and I'll teach you how to shop like Massie."

"Why?" Ripple sat up; this time, her tone was unmistakably full of questions. "Who do you like?"

"No one." Kristen fanned her cheeks. "I have a costume party next weekend and—"

"Is it Jax?" Ripple's light brown eyes were full of insecurity, not cattiness. And for a split second, Kristen took pleasure in the idea that another girl might consider her a threat. Too bad that other girl wasn't Skye.

"It's not Jax."

"Scooter?"

"No."

"Tyler?"

"No."

"Cam?"

"No."

"Plovert?"

"No."

"Josh?"

"Stop!" Kristen shouted. Getting interrogated by a nine-year-old was more humiliating than wearing an old head trend (in poo brown!) to impress a boy who wasn't even home.

Ripple was silent while she considered the other possibilities. "Who else do you know who skates?" And then she slapped her hand against her goopy lips. "Noooo!"

Kristen nodded shyly.

"Massie's crush? Derek Harrington?" Ripple widened her narrow eyes as much as she possibly could.

"Gawd, no! It's Dune!" Kristen accidentally blurted. It was all she could do to keep the little wannabe from thinking she'd ever, in a billion years, steal her alpha's crush.

"My brother?" Ripple screeched, as if they had been talking about Shrek.

"Yeah." Kristen peeked down at the driveway to make sure no one had been listening. "Now will you help me?"

"Yeah," Ripple said as she eyed Kristen's pasty legs. "Someone's got to."

The twenty-seven dollars Kristen spent on the cab ride to the new Roxy/Quiksilver store was almost half of what she'd made during her short career as a tutor-sitter. But as she saw it, the money was an investment in her future. A future she could no longer imagine without her CLAM crush.

After a quick sweat swipe with the nubby coral towel, both girls decided their new "thems" couldn't wait for a shower and wardrobe change. They wanted to be transformed immediately. So off they went covered in little more than sarongs and SPF 30.

"Are you sure this is the best place?" Kristen asked Ripple as she clutched the mini-surfboard door handle and stepped inside the Hawaiian-themed boutique. The blast of air-conditioning rendered her red and orange wrap useless and made the blond hair on her arms stand up.

"Trust me." Ripple led her to the back of the store where giant colorful posters of sunny girls with cute braids and sea-sprayed bangs charged giant waves in bright bikinis. Their simple lifestyles suddenly made the pads, cleats, and unflattering kneesocks of soccer seem stinky and un-cute.

"May I help you?" asked a glitter-dusted Asian girl with

a perky grin and a pricing gun. She wore faded denim short shorts, a yellow tube top, and a pink lei around her neck, which suddenly seemed ten times more creative and alluring than Kristen's conservative Coach locket. Brightly colored cotton in fun, girly prints swirled all around her, the fabrics looking as light and giddy as the girls they were designed for. And suddenly Kristen longed to be one of them. She longed to be satisfied by a beautiful day at the beach. To be tickled by her whimsical wardrobe. To be riding in a beat-up old car with no AC, her sand-covered, home-polished toes sticking out the windows. She longed to be free. She longed to be Roxy.

"Can you show us your baggy cargo shorts and—"

Kristen snapped back to reality at the sound of Ripple's pinched voice and grabbed her by the wrist. "We're okay, thanks," she told the salesgirl.

"Kewl," said the girl as she gladly punched a SALE sticker on a pair of silver skull–covered board shorts.

"Rule number one," Kristen hissed. "If you want to shop like Massie, never ask for help. Make them think *you're* the expert."

Ripple hyper-nodded. "What else?"

Kristen pulled her down onto a bright blue leather couch by the dressing room and leaned in. She was about to reveal Massie's trade secrets and couldn't risk being overheard. Not even by the nearby mannequin in the rainbow-striped bikini.

"Rule number two. Never check price tags. Act like you have endless amounts of cash."

"What if you don't?" Ripple squeaked.

Kristen fought the urge to hug the girl, who at that moment could have been a younger version of herself.

"Peek at the price in the dressing room," Kristen whisper-advised. "If it's too expensive, ask for it in a color you know they don't make."

"I thought we weren't supposed to ask for help." Ripple's narrow eyes were wide again.

"That's outside the dressing room. Once you're inside, you should ask for help all the time. Make them *work* for you."

Ripple nodded like she was finally starting to catch on.

"When deciding between two sizes, always try the bigger one on first. That way you get to parade through the store in something that's too big, asking for a smaller size. The fat people will be totally jealous."

Ripple licked her lips, eating it all up.

"Oh, and skin is in." Kristen suddenly recalled the last thing Massie had e-mailed the Pretty Committee before leaving for riding camp. "The more you show, the better."

"Like, how much skin?" Ripple slid her hands under her butt. Her sweaty palms rubbed against the leather seat of the couch and made a low farting sound that neither of them acknowledged. The moment was too serious.

"As much as you can afford, I guess."

Ripple crinkled her brows in confusion.

"Snakeskin," Kristen clarified. "Nawt Ripple-skin. Now me. What does Dune like?" She stood and flip-flopped over to a rack of breezy feminine dresses full of fresh colors, playful patterns, and fetching adornments like heart-shaped buttons and braided straps. "What about this one?" She pulled an orange T-shirt dress off the rack that had white dandelions stitched across the bottom. In the poster on the far wall it had been paired with chunky turquoise beaded bracelets. The sight alone would have given Massie a rash. But it filled Kristen with the buzz of springtime. And springtime filled everyone with love—even surfers.

"Dune likes gray," Ripple said flatly. Her announcement felt like the arrival of storm clouds at a Fourth of July barbecue. Ripple held up a pair of knee-length cargoes covered in more pockets than a Kipling backpack. "I would put it with one of these." She offered a dull beige racer-back tank and a faded red short-sleeve hoodie.

"Really?" Kristen asked, letting go of the dress. It swung back into place on the bar with the other girly dresses to the teasing schoolyard tune *neh-neh-neh-neh-nehhhh, you ca-ann't-have-meeeee.* After a few more mocking swings, Kristen finally punched it.

With little enthusiasm, she tried on the shorts and the red hoodie (at least it had *some* color) and found that, unfortunately, they fit.

"He's gonna love them." Ripple clapped her hands together

like an overly zealous wardrobe stylist. "Now, let's go buy some skin."

"Sounds good." Kristen did her best to sound upbeat. She even managed to smile when she handed the cashier the last of her tutor-sitting money—a move that would have been a lot less painful had she bought the cute orange dress.

But it was too late.

She was now the proud owner of a baggy outfit in drab winter colors that made her look more like Cesario than Viola. And, according to the receipt in her clammy hand, all sales were final.

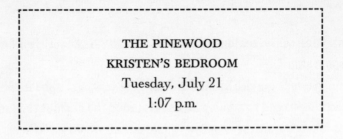

Kristen was already seven minutes late for GAS Park when the backside of her silver Guess Carousel watch beeped.

Ugh!

She locked her bedroom door, pulled her laptop out of David Beckham's kitty litter, stuck in the code key, and quickly slapped on her Cleopatra wig. There was no time for a wardrobe change, so instead of wearing the white Greek goddess dress, she tilted the computer's camera up, hoping no one would notice her baggy gray cargo shorts and faded red hoodie.

The screen came to life. And the members of the Witty Committee stared back at their alpha.

EINSTEIN (Layne Abeley)	**BILL GATES (Danh Bondok)**
Disguise: tweed coat, bushy mustache, wiry gray wig	**Disguise:** glasses, light blue button-down, dark blue blazer
Expertise: physics	**Expertise:** technology
OPRAH (Rachel Walker)	**SHAKESPEARE (Aimee Snyder)**
Disguise: wavy black wig, gold hoop earrings, pumpkin orange blouse	**Disguise:** gray bald-in-the-front, curly-in-the-back wig, mustache, white collar sticking out of a black cloak
Expertise: anthropology (the study of humankind, not the cute and affordable shabby-chic store)	**Expertise:** affairs of the heart and the Romance languages

"What do we stand for?" Kristen asked, never tiring of the routine.

"BOB," they answered.

"And what does BOB stand for?"

"Brains over beauty!"

She smiled, her stress melting like Creamsicle-flavored Glossip Girl in the sun. Nothing validated her more than the WC, not even David Beckham's loving neck licks.

"State the reason for this meeting," Kristen insisted in her best robot-meets-no-nonsense-CEO voice.

"We've been waiting for a progress report and never got one." Oprah fiddled nervously with one gold hoop earring.

"Did you take my advice? Did you and Ripple help each other?"

"Looks like it," Einstein snickered, straining to see beyond the camera's reach. "What are you *wearing*?"

"Hey, are those shorts from Quiksilver?" Bill Gates asked, nudging his round glasses a little farther up his shiny nose. "I have the same pair."

"You shop in the girls' section?" Kristen asked.

"No, you shop in the *boys'*," he countered. "B-but they look good on you. I mean, you know, you can totally pull them off."

"You wish," Shakespeare muttered.

Einstein and Oprah giggled.

Bill Gates turned red.

"Wait!" he screeched. "I didn't mean it like *that*. I meant—"

"It's okay." Kristen hurried him along, angling the computer even farther up. "I *know* what you meant. And thanks for checking in, but I'm fine. . . . Actually, I'm late. Dune is at GAS Park right now, so I better go."

"Question." Oprah's round dark eyes seized Kristen, refusing to let her go. "Is that what you're wearing?"

Kristen nodded yes.

"Then we'll get moving on plan B right away," Oprah announced.

"What's plan B?" Kristen asked. "Why are we moving to it? I never approved it."

"Because I'm not so sure plan A is working."

Kristen, about to protest, looked down at her outfit and sighed. She couldn't argue with that. But Ripple had sworn by the dude-duds. And when it came to Dune, she was smarter than any of them. . . .

Right?

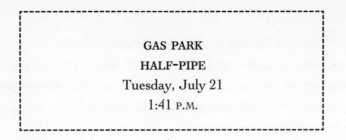

The way Kristen threw her leg over her bike, with uninhibited force, gave her pause. Usually she slid back on the gold banana seat, lifted on to her left toes, and swung her leg over with grace and modesty. Then she'd lower down and roll back her shoulders with the posture of a world-class gymnast. But something about the long, baggy shorts, formless sweatshirt, and fat black DC sneakers made her feel more lad and less lady. And she ambled into GAS Park with the side-to-side swagger to prove it.

Skaters greeted her with respectful head-nods when she passed. Not because she was hawt, but because she was nawt. She was no longer a pretty blonde who could knock them off their boards with a suggestive half smile or a whiff of her citrus-scented body oil. Kristen was suddenly a girl they could hang around without feeling conscious of their back zits (bacne) or their mid-afternoon BO.

She was a buddy, not a beauty.

The realization was enough to make her want to hop back on her bike and pedal to the nearest Bebe. But she had no money, and even less time. Skye and the DSL Daters were all over Dune like SPF 50.

Kristen hiked up her shorts and hurried over to greet them. They were in the juniors' area, surrounded by young boys in helmets who were rolling down little asphalt hills with their tongues sticking out of their mouths. Despite the cramped course, no one dared complain. Because for the first time ever, GAS had been invaded by hawt blondes in bikinis. For the first time, they were getting a taste of what was missing in their lives.

"Hey." Kristen greeted Dune, Tyler, and Jax with a confident smile, ignoring the fact that they were in the middle of helping the wobbly-on-purpose DSL Daters balance on their new pink boards. Scooter, however, was zipping past the little skater guys with roller-derby determination. Ripple was there too, and she seemed particularly interested in tips from Jax, even though the pictures in her bedroom showed her charging the half-pipe without protective gear. No one stopped to say hi, except—

"Hey, Kristen." Dune turned to face her, and suddenly the unnerving rumble of wheels scraping along the pavement faded into the background. His navy T-shirt was off—stuffed down the back of his red checked surf trunks—and his feet were bare and golden brown.

"What are you doing here?" He stepped away from his friends so he could welcome-touch her shoulder. It was either a flirty gesture or a subtle attempt to see if she was *really* wearing a sweatshirt in the middle of July.

"Tutoring." Kristen chin-pointed at Ripple, who was

comparing tan lines with the short DSL Dater in the white string bikini and black mesh cover-up.

"In what?" Dune rolled his eyes behind his sister's back. "Selling out and acting like a different person to impress a guy?"

Kristen felt herself blush. Was he accusing her of doing the same thing or just annoyed by his new and *un*-improved sister? Either way, Kristen didn't have an answer for him. At least not one that didn't make her seem like a skater-stalker. So she ignored his question and went to greet her "student."

"Ready to hit the books?" Kristen slapped Ripple on the butt, aware of how dorky her entrance was. It was the first time she'd ever butt-slapped anyone or said "hit the books." But her heart was all aflutter and sending unreliable information to her brain.

"No thanks," Ripple muttered dismissively, as if Kristen was an annoying waitress, wondering if she'd like a sixth refill on her soda. Then she turned to Jax and rolled her eyes.

"Laundry day?" Skye jumped off her pink board and stretched her hammy. She glared at the gray cargoes and lifted her blond brows. But Kristen was too consumed with Skye's outfit to care.

"Where did you get that?" Kristen asked the orange T-shirt dress with the daisies across the bottom.

Skye tossed her hair over her shoulders. "Quiksilver/

Roxy," she said, like it was someplace she shopped all the time, even though everyone knew she only wore clothes from her parents' boutique at the Body Alive Dance Studio.

"Rassssssie." Kristen pulled Ripple off Jax's board and yanked her close so no one could hear. "Please tell me that the dress thing is a coincidence." Her voice shook. She didn't need an answer to know she had been betrayed.

"It was the weirdest thing." Ripple twirled the turquoise Roxy beaded bracelets around her wrists—the same ones Skye was wearing. Only Ripple had paired them with a bold green shift dress that had white blades of grass rising up from the hem. "Right after we said goodbye, Skye called and asked me to take her shopping. Turns out she has the same taste in boys as you do."

Kristen's mouth went dry.

"And you *took* her?" she managed.

"At first I said no because I thought it might be unfair to you." Ripple tightened her high, parched ponytail. "But then she offered to buy me an outfit, so . . ."

Sweat started to trickle down Kristen's back. "So why didn't you tell her to get *these*?" She hate-tugged her shorts.

"Because you bought the last pair."

Kristen's skin prickled and her legs twitched. Pre-soccer-game-like adrenaline zipped through her body, begging her to get physical. If she didn't kick something or run some-where, she'd explode. But the only open field was on the other side of the fence—and she wasn't a member. So she dug her home-manicured nails in her palms and willed herself not to pummel her crush's baby sister.

"I quit!" Kristen blurted, opting for the verbal beat-down.

"Too late." Ripple smirked, crossing her arms over her green dress. "I already fired you this morning."

"What?" Kristen hissed, suddenly grateful that Dune and his friends were too distracted by the DSL Daters to realize she was getting worked by an LBR nine-year-old with wannabe issues.

"Yeah, I told my dad math finally clicked and that I was done."

"Why?"

"I want to have fun." Ripple shrugged as if it should have been obvious. "And no offense, Ms. Gregory, but *this*"—she pointed from Kristen to herself and back to Kristen again— "is not, not, *not* fun."

"Who wanted to try doubles?" Jax called from the half-pipe.

"Meeeeee." Ripple tossed her hair over her shoulders the way Skye always did, then hurried away.

Kristen shock-stood off to the side of the park, watching her crush flirt with a blond alpha in a dress *she* had wanted to buy. Skye was bragging about sneaking into the country club after hours and going for illegal midnight swims. The sheer daring of it made Dune's light brown eyes get even lighter. The he told her about his illegal phosphorescent surf and gladly returned her oh-my-gawd-we-are-like-sooo-much-the-same hug.

Standing solo, wearing temperature-inappropriate clothes, envy and longing seeping from her sweat-clogged pores, Kristen felt like a party-LBR. The kind who always stared at the Pretty Committee as if weighing her choices—*Hmmmm, I could try and join in the fun, or slash them to death with my cuticle-clipper key chain.*

After they finished hugging, Skye changed topics and began bragging about some ultra-exclusive performing arts boarding school called Alphas that she had applied for. Kristen started to search Dune's face for hints of sadness at the possibility of Skye leaving town, but her cell phone vibrated before she could get an accurate reading.

Kristen dug deep into her pocket and checked her phone. One new text message:

Your shoelace is undone. Tie it!

She quickly scanned GAS Park, in case one of Dune's friends was trying to sucker punch her. But they were too captivated by the bikini blondes to bother with jokes.

Then came a follow-up text:

Now!

And without another thought, Kristen crouched down and reached for her very tied, very tight laces. She was about to stand when she heard someone yell, "I've been hit!"

Kristen looked up just as a mass of white golf balls sailed over the fence and rained down on GAS Park like a plague of locusts.

"Owwww!"

"Oof!"

"What the . . . ?!"

"My back!"

"My coccyx!"

The cries of pain did not stop until the last ball settled on the pavement.

Finally, all was silent. But one by one, the skaters rose like zombies shaking off the night fog and hungry for revenge.

"Spies!" shouted a boy as he picked up a golf ball and whipped it at an abandoned pink DSL Dater board.

"Terrorists!" shouted another young boy in head-to-toe pads, nursing a bloody nose.

"Get 'em!" someone else yelled.

"AHHHHH!"

Kristen took cover under the brown wood roof of the snack shack as a flurry of balls forced the intruders to shriek loudly, kick off their sandals, and climb like Spider-Men back over the fence. They didn't stop until Ripple and her mirrored makeup caddy had joined them.

Once they were gone, everyone applauded—even Dune, Jax, and Tyler. Kristen clapped her palms raw and didn't stop until another text buzzed through to her phone.

Offer payback. Meet @ the CC 11 P.M. Tonight. Instructions
will be with your doorman.

Kristen quickly deleted the message, then approached
Dune.

"Wanna get them back?" she offered calmly as her baggy
boy shorts flapped in the breeze.

Dune slowly nodded yes, as if still in shock. Seconds later
the light in his eyes seemed to reappear, like a blackout that
had suddenly ended. And under that light it didn't matter if
Kristen was wearing the same shorts as Bill Gates. She felt
pretty again.

"Guys, listen to this." He waved over his buddies, who
surrounded Kristen like hungry sharks.

"Meet me at the country club service entrance at eleven
o'clock tonight," she whispered. "Make sure you're not being
followed. I have to go get ready."

"What's the plan?" Tyler asked. "How do we know it's
gonna work?"

"Do *you* have any ideas?" Dune challenged his buddy.

"Yeah, but most of them are illegal." He snickered. "Is
yours?"

"Probably," Kristen said with fake nonchalance.

Dune put his arm on Kristen's shoulder. Her back sweat
returned.

"I'm not crazy about your clothes, but I love the way you think."

Kristen half smiled. Because half of his declaration was a whole lot nicer than anything a hawt boy had ever said to her.

Every time Kristen pictured herself dressed in those horrible boy clothes, she pedaled her bike a little faster, as if she could somehow liquefy the embarrassing memory and sweat it out through her pores.

Not that her current outfit was much better.

There had been a lot of things she'd had to keep in mind when selecting that night's ensemble. It had to be:

A) Dark and unassuming for her secret mission.

B) Flattering enough to make Dune forget he ever saw her kick it Cesario-style.

C) Conservative enough for her mother to believe she was rushing out to help Ripple cram for a math quiz.

D) Comfortable enough for her to crouch behind a bush for four hours while she: 1) Waited for everyone to show up. (Her mother would never let her go out at 11 p.m., so she'd had to leave at 7 p.m. and hide out.) 2) Figured out how to use the Witty Committee's invention.

E) Something that had not yet received the OCDiva

treatment (e.g., replacing cheap plastic with Chanel buttons).

F) Narrow enough to keep her pant legs from getting stuck in the bike chain.

G) Free of David Beckham fur. Nothing says *I smell like cat pee* like a girl covered in hair balls.

H) All of the above. ✓

After intense analysis, Kristen had decided on a long black Juicy tunic hoodie (Massie hand-me-down) over gray denim capris (Old Navy, to be destroyed by "accidental pen explosion" one week before the Pretty Committee returned). Black ballet flats (Capezio sale bin—seven dollars!) completed the vandal-chic look she was going for. She'd considered wearing her Cleopatra wig, not only for the pop it gave her green eyes, but for its ability to conceal her blond hair. Ultimately, though, she'd decided against it. Because the only thing Kristen wanted more than to make Dune fall in love with her was to keep the Witty Committee secret. They could always cheer her up if she lost Dune, but *he* could never fill the void if she lost them. No one could. So tonight, her blond hair was stuffed under a Burton snowboard cap. As she urged her bike forward, she pedal-prayed the combination of extreme humidity and black wool would not make her forehead break out in the morning.

Kristen got off her bike three blocks away from the country club and locked it to a burned-out streetlight. She checked left, then right. Certain no one was watching, she lifted the flap on her leather saddlebag (a gift from her uncle Billy in Texas) and pulled out the clear backpack. The pink crystals inside made it too heavy to wear, so she carried it in her arms like a big, crippled dog and waddled down the dark sidewalk like a pregnant penguin.

For the next three and a half hours, Kristen hid behind the shrub next to the service gate and studied the instructions the Witty Committee had left in the outside pocket of her backpack. They weren't complicated. In fact, their simplicity was brilliant.

As her legs cramped from crouching and her stomach grumbled from a Ziploc dinner of milkless Lucky Charms (for luck), Kristen thought—fleetingly—about bailing. She was not a rule breaker by nature. Sure, she wore cute clothes behind her mother's back and let the PC copy her homework, but nothing illegal. Ever! Yet here she was, about to trespass and vandalize. In a place she loved going to with Massie and the Blocks. And that should have made her feel awkward and uneasy, like she had in those boy clothes. But for some reason it didn't. Instead it felt:

A) Exhilarating.
B) Daring.
C) Empowering.
D) Romantic.
E) All of the above. ✓

It felt like she was about to face *her* mega-wave and find out what she was made of. After years of hiding behind Massie, her mother, her homework, and her soccer coach, Kristen was ready times ten for the answer.

"Ripple, come awn!" Dune's terse whisper cut through the muggy summer night like a beautifully polished knife through red velvet cake—bringing her one step closer to pure heaven.

Kristen brushed the dirt off her butt and stood. Why get caught in the poop-in-the-woods position unless it was absolutely necessary? Which it wasn't. The staff had left over twenty minutes ago and the club was deserted.

Tyler, Jax, and Scooter shuffled along a few paces behind Dune, their hands stuffed in the pockets of their skinny jeans and their shoulders slumped toward the dirt road. Ripple, a few paces behind them, was teetering on platform espadrilles, texting and chew-snapping a wad of brown Bubblicious.

"Ahhhh, smell that?" Dune sniffed the lobster bisque–scented air.

Kristen giggled, to show Dune she was ready to have fun despite their risky agenda.

"It's the sweet smell of revenge." He put his arm around her shoulders, then quickly removed it. The brief contact was enough to make the ends of her straight blond hair curl.

"I thought it was Jax," Tyler chuckled.

"What?" Jax whisper-screeched.

"Sucker punch!" Tyler nudged him with his black plaster cast.

"Shhhhh." Kristen lifted her French manicured nail to her lips, casually showing off her flawless home job.

Ripple popped a bubble against her glossy mouth.

Kristen glared at her, making it perfectly clear who was running this operation. Ripple gently peeled the gum off her face and tossed the wad in the bushes.

Kristen let the un-green gesture slide and continued whispering. "Security patrols the grounds constantly. But there are only two guys, and it takes them exactly nineteen minutes to walk the periphery," she explained, having memorized the Witty Committee's instructions. "Which means we have to get in and get out—fast."

Dune grin-nodded, then turned to look at his friends in an I-told-you-she-was-cool sort of way.

And that gave Kristen the strength to continue playing alpha even though the position hadn't officially been handed to her yet.

"There are five valves that control the sprinkler system. They are located to the right of the laundry room." She pointed at the white woodshed about fifty yards away. "I'll dump the color crystals in the water tank—on my cue, you turn the dials. And if all goes well"—Kristen paused for dramatic emphasis—"the *green* will be *pink* by morning."

"Genius!" Dune punched the starry sky.

"Cool." Tyler and Jax snickered.

Even Scooter allowed himself to smile. But Ripple ignored them all and kept texting.

"Why are you here if you're not going to pay attention?" Kristen hissed in Ripple's faux diamond–studded ear.

"My tutor-sitter was fired today and my dad is out." She smirked.

Kristen summoned her love of Dune to stop herself from pulling his sister's dry "before" hair out of her scalp.

The crunch of wheels on gravel sounded from the distance.

"Look, the guards," Jax gasped, pointing his skull-ringed index figure at a black SUV.

Kristen's heart started rattling around in her chest, but she took a deep, calming breath, flipped her watch to the LCD side, and set the timer. If she gave the cops four minutes to pass, they'd still have nine minutes to get the job done and six more for travel.

"Shhh. We're fine," Kristen whisper-hissed. According to the plan, it was totally doable.

They sat in total silence with nothing but the distant *whoosh* of passing cars and the sound of their heartbeats to keep them entertained.

"Let's go," Kristen said once the guards had passed. She lifted her heavy pack with a grunt. Without a word, Dune took it and strapped it to his back, like it was made of weightless fairy dust. Free of weight and full of love, Kristen led the way toward the club's PRIVATE PROPERTY sign with the swift sprint of a seasoned soccer captain.

They all managed to scale the fence without a problem, except Ripple, who was faux-struggling, obviously hoping Jax would help her. But there was no time for games.

"Skye scales the fence into GAS all the time. It's totally alpha," Kristen whispered after landing on the other side. And before she knew it, Ripple was by her side.

As she led the way to the shed, the bottoms of Kristen's feet throbbed from stepping on the chain link in her flats. But she didn't care.

Love was supposed to hurt.

Kristen's WC skeleton key (thank you, Einstein!) unlocked the shed door and earned her a round of supportive back pats from the boys. If happiness were bricks and stones, she'd have been the Great Wall of China.

The giant silver water tank was in the middle of the shed, humming and bubbling just like the WC had said it would be. But no one had warned her about the skunk smell, which for some reason she found embarrassing, even though she had nothing to do with it.

The gleaming sprinkler valves jetted out of the tank as if begging to be turned—begging to be used in a way they had never been used before. Begging to see what they were truly made of. And Kristen winked at them, as though they were old friends who, after all these years, still had everything in common.

"Okay, everyone grab a dial and I'll—"

"You gotta get outta here!" a girl panted behind them.

Everyone turned to find Skye standing in the doorway, the full moon illuminating her pewter metallic bikini as if moonlight came free with purchase. A tangle of jewel-toned gauze scarves were tied around her long neck, drawing attention to her bone-deep tan and white blond curls. Her abs were more chiseled than Ashlee Simpson's nose. She looked annoyingly airbrushed.

Kristen's insides were jumping up and down shouting, *Whyyyy meeeeee?* But her thick skin kept the others from hearing it.

"Huh?" Jax stared at her shiny B-cups, looking slightly dazed.

"I was about to go for my midnight swim when I heard the guards on their walkie-talkies. You guys were spotted on the security cameras. They're on their way!"

"What cameras?" Kristen challenged. The blueprints never showed any. . . .

Ripple nervously chewed the gloss off her lower lip as she discreetly slid her cell phone into the front pocket of her denim Roxy minidress.

"Do you want to obsess over cameras, or do you want me to get you out of here?"

"How awesome are you?" Dune asked Skye, dropping Kristen's backpack in a corner.

"We can talk about *me* later," Skye said in a totally self-obsessed serious way. "Follow me."

The guys seemed more than happy to run behind Skye—

after all, it was a free invitation to watch her dancer's butt in a metallic bikini for fifty yards without being called out on it. Kristen, however, chose to speed-walk her way to safety, refusing to completely buy Skye's story and double-refusing to accept that *Skye* would be crowned heroine of the night.

Ugh. Kristen was surfing a wave of j-barf.

"Here they come," Skye whisper-shouted. "There's a break in the fence by that rock. We can fit under so they don't see us hop the barrier."

"Are you *sure*?" Kristen challenged, hoping to expose her as a fraud.

"How do you think I get in here every night?" the alpha whisper-shot back.

"Point!" Kristen could practically hear Alicia say.

Skye checked over her shoulder then lifted the torn metal like a curtain. "Non-members first," she insisted with a sacrificing smile. "You'll be in a lot more trouble than I will if you get caught."

"How cool is she?" Jax mumbled to his boys as they belly-crawled through the dirt like soldiers at boot camp.

Kristen fake-coughed, hoping to drown out Dune's response. It worked, but his brow-lift plus thumbs-up said it all.

Everyone but Skye and Kristen had made it through when they heard the stealth hum of a golf cart.

"Come awn!" urged the survivors from the safe side. "Hurry!"

Knowing this was her only chance to out alpha-Skye, Kristen did the honorable thing and took a step back.

"This was *my* mission," she said loud enough to remind everyone. "If anyone goes down for this, it should be me. You go first."

"But it's *my* rescue, so *you* should go first!"

Circles of light danced around them like morbidly obese fireflies. "Who's there?" called a security guard, frantically waving his flashlight.

"Hurry!" Kristen said. The bottoms of her feet were tingling, anxious to get moving. Anxious to show the others what years of soccer drills could do for a girl. "There's time for both of us to make it if you go *now*," she whisper-shouted. "Go." She gently shoved Skye onto the ground and foot-nudged her toward the opening in the fence . . . not because she had dreamed of doing that from the moment they met. It was to save her, of course.

"Ow!" Skye whined, mostly for the sake of the boys, who were watching the mini catfight as if it were the Super Bowl.

The lights were getting closer and the jingle of keys was getting louder. "Stop!" shout-coughed a man who was fighting a losing battle with bronchitis.

Kristen was too afraid to turn around, but she could tell by the sound of his voice that she still had a few seconds before he could grab her arm or ID her face. She crouched down, preparing to crawl, but Skye was still under the fence. "Go!"

"I can't," Skye panicked. "My scarf is stuck."

"Hurry!" Ripple called.

"Let's go!" Dune urged.

"I'm trying," Skye grunted.

Kristen frantically ran her hands along the metal diamonds, searching for the snag. "I don't feel anything."

"You *don't*?" Skye's devious smirk was suddenly illuminated by the security guard's flashlight. "Ooops." She slid under the fence like a greased sardine. "My bad."

"What?!" Kristen was about to accuse Skye of sabotage, but she was yanked to her feet with such force that the words fell out of her mouth and landed in the dirt. Just like the rest of her night.

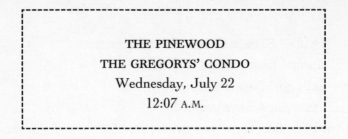

Marsha Gregory yanked open the front door before Dwight, the security guard, had a chance to ring the bell. She was wearing a red paisley pajama set and beige Ugg slippers, and her mousy brown bob was pulled into a tiny ponytail. Her creamy skin was soft with night cream, making her hard green eyes look like two sharp rocks in an otherwise glistening stream.

"Who is *this*?" She glared at Dwight's bushy mustache with contempt and pulled her daughter inside. "I thought you said you were sleeping at Ripple's house? Why are you covered in mud? Where's your bike? Is your scholarship in jeopardy?"

Even though being escorted home in a security car that smelled like McDonald's pickles and had crackly jazz music playing through its garbled speakers had been an all-time low, Kristen was grateful she had a witness. Someone who could verify in a court of law if need be that her mother tended toward the hysterical.

"My name is Dwight Wolcott, and I found your daughter trespassing at the Westchester Country Club." He stuck his chubby red nose a little further inside the Pine-Sol–scented

foyer. After a quick evaluation of the distressed wood cre-
denza, straw wall-hangings from Pier 1 Imports, and the
glistening plastic plants that tried their very hardest to look
real, he cleared his phlegm-filled throat and smirked. "And
something tells me you're not members."

"Really, Dwight, and you *are*?" Marsha folded her arms
across her braless chest.

Kristen wanted to hug her mother and hide at the
same time. She loved how easy it was for Marsha to hold
on to her pride and own who she was. But at the same
time, she wished it hadn't been necessary. For once it
would have been nice to know that their lifestyle didn't
need defending. And that they could be accepted just the
way they were.

Dwight coughed and quickly checked his walkie-talkie
as if it were a direct line to the president. "I better be
going. . . ." He jammed it back onto his brown belt, which
looked terrible, by the way, with his all-black uniform.

"Yes." Marsha put a protective arm around her daughter.
"You better."

Kristen smirked at Dwight, like a spoiled girl whose parents never punished her. But that was merely a fantasy—
a fantasy that would only last until they heard the hallway
elevator doors close. As soon as they did, Kristen's worst
fears would be confirmed.

"Explain." Marsha tucked a loose hair behind her ear and
glared at her daughter.

Kristen inhaled sharply, hoping something would come to her by the time she exhaled. But it wasn't necessary.

"You're done," her mother snapped before she could speak. "I thought there wasn't going to be any more trouble after your expulsion from OCD. I thought your life was going to be school and soccer. Isn't that what you told me?"

"I was just—"

"Trespassing? Lying to your mother? Playing Russian roulette with your free pass to the most prestigious middle school on the East Coast?"

Kristen lowered her eyes. The parquet floorboards blurred through her tears—tears she cried not so much over her impending punishment but over her inability to do what other kids did and get away with it. It was like she had one of those invisible dog fences around her body, and every time she did something that went against her good-girl nature, she got zapped. Why didn't the Pretty Committee or Skye or Dune or Ripple have invisible fences around *them*? Why could they break the rules and still come out smiling? Why was Kristen being forced into a lifetime of perfection?

"You are grounded for the rest of the summer. That means no—"

A light rap on the door interrupted her. It was probably Dwight, who'd just received word that her red crystal–filled backpack had been discovered in the maintenance shack, the final piece of evidence needed to land her a life sentence. The rest of her education would come from the bloodstained pages of prison library books and CNN on a TV the size of a toaster.

"Yes, Dwight," Marsha said with an I-am-more-than-qualified-to-take-it-from-here huff.

But the opposite of Dwight was standing in their doorway.

It was Dune.

Kristen's stomach lurched. A cute, shirtless boy whose idea of "school" consisted of several fish swimming by his surfboard at the same time could only worsen this horrible situation.

"Hi, Mrs. Gregory, I'm Dune."

Kristen's mom glowered at him the same way she always eyed the skinny girl who worked at the smoothie shop, silently insisting that they keep squeezing until every last drop of juice was drained from the fruit and in her to-go cup.

And, like the skinny girl at the shop, Dune eventually got the hint.

"I just wanted to come here and thank your daughter for trying to save my little sister."

Kristen and Marsha raised their eyebrows.

"She was tutoring Ripple when Ripple snuck out to the country club. Kristen went after her to bring her home before she got in trouble or . . ." He paused for effect, shaking his head grimly. "Or worse. Anyway, my sister got away, but your thoughtful daughter didn't. And on behalf of my grateful father, who is waiting downstairs in the car, we just want to thank you for raising such a responsible girl."

Marsha looked at her daughter, silently asking if this was true. Kristen dried her tears on her black sleeve and nodded yes. Next thing she knew, she was being swept into a Bounce fabric softener–scented embrace, smiling into a fold of paisley-covered faux-satin.

Without another word, or even a thank you to Dune, Marsha released Kristen, turned in her Uggs, and shuffled down the parquet hallway toward her bedroom. It was her way of letting Kristen know that she trusted her again. And as for Dune, Marsha owed him nothing. Allowing him five minutes of alone time with her daughter after dark was thanks enough.

"Ehmagawd." Kristen mouthed her gratitude. Not only for saving her, but for finally showing her that he was really, truly crushing back—a gesture far more romantic than diamonds or taking a private jet to Paris for dinner. She made a mental note to return the favor times ten, so he'd know there was no question that she felt the same way he did. But for now, a humble show of appreciation would do.

Kristen touched his arm gently. "I can't believe you did that for me."

"Of course." He nervously gathered his blond hair like he was going to tie it back and then let it go. "I never leave a buddy behind. Number one rule of surfing."

Kristen felt a sharp sting under her armpits when he said

buddy, but she filed it under "surf term." It probably meant something closer to soul mates, *right*?

"And how unbelievably awesome is it to have *Skye* in our group? People never think that super-hot girls can be cool, but she proves them wrong, don'tcha think?" His round pupils turned to hearts whenever he said *her* name.

Meanwhile, Kristen's heart took a running leap off the Gregorys' fifth-floor balcony and smashed on the pavement of the visitors' parking lot below. She forced a smile, but it probably looked more like a crooked line. "You better go."

"Seriously." He chuckled. "Skye is at my house, watching Ripple. If I don't get back soon, the walls will be covered in glitter nail polish." He chuckled again. "Aren't girly girls funny?"

Kristen wanted to grab him by the shoulders and tell him that *she* was into glitter polish. That *she* was a girly girl. That *she* was funny! And that if she'd had the confidence to ignore Ripple's terrible advice, she would have been wearing the orange dress with the turquoise bracelets. But all she did was thank him again and close the door.

The rest she would save for a box of Puffs and David Beckham.

Marsha stopped her silver Toyota Prius in front of the valet parking attendant with the confidence of Paris Hilton's chauffeur.

A Hayden Christensen look-alike in white Bermuda shorts and a matching white button-down jogged over with an eager smile that said, *I'll pretend your Prius is a Mercedes if you tip me well.*

But Marsha's hand was nowhere near her generic black pleather wallet. It was on her daughter's knee—disguised as an act of affection but really checking for stubble to see if Kristen was in violation of the no-shaving-until-you're-fifteen rule.

Kristen crossed her illegal leg and sighed. "This isn't necessary, Mom."

On the other side of the window, Hayden Christensen was holding on to his smile as best he could. But it couldn't have been easy considering Marsha refused to acknowledge him and that a shiny red Jaguar convertible had just pulled up behind them.

"It *is* necessary." The sharp corners of Marsha's bob swung forward with the force of her conviction. "The club made a terrible mistake in vilifying you when you were only trying to help. Their manager owes you an apology. And I spent all morning on the phone making sure you'll get it."

A wave of vertigo caught Kristen off guard. Her insides rose and sank like she was back on Dune's board, riding the gentle, lapping surf of the sound. Only this time the churning in her stomach came from depression, not the promise of love. She angled the air-conditioning vent toward her face and inhaled deeply. It was impossible to know if her mother's intentions were pure or just another game of chicken.

More often than not, Marsha would *act* like she was on her daughter's side, knowing the guilt would eventually break her, and she'd confess. And she was usually right. But not today. Kristen was friendless, jobless, and crushless. It was crucial for her fading self-esteem that she win *something*—or the only thing she'd have to show for her summer was a PhD in Advanced LBR.

Hayden knuckle-tapped the window.

Marsha, refusing to let her precious AC seep onto country club property, where they had "more than enough to go around," faced the closed glass and mouthed, "I'll park myself. We're not staying long."

She turned to Kristen with renewed purpose. "I'll meet you back here in fifteen minutes. See if he'll give you a free membership."

Kristen grabbed the door handle, hoping that in the next millisecond something divine might happen and interrupt the next fifteen minutes of her life. But unfortunately, the sun was still shining down on the hunter green awnings of the country club. And the cars lined up behind them were honking impatiently.

"I'm really glad things turned out the way they did." Marsha grinned as Kristen stepped out of the Prius. "I would have hated to punish you for the entire eighth grade. And I would have *had* to. You know that, *right*?" She smiled and waved goodbye to her daughter. "See you at one forty-five." She tapped the digital clock on the dash with her buffed nail.

"'Kay." Kristen closed the door a little harder than an innocent person would have.

The club's foyer was dark in a way that's pleasing only to rich people. Kristen could barely see the outline of the slight blonde behind the semicircular mahogany reception desk. She was backlit by a sunbeam that had managed to squeeze through the open porthole-shaped window behind her—the only source of light in a room dotted with leather club chairs, green carpeting, and maroon velvet curtains. The beam, like Kristen, was there on borrowed time.

"Member number?" Her raspy voice sawed through the steak-scented foyer like a worn nail file.

Suddenly, Kristen felt dirty in her navy racer-back T-shirt dress and silver Pumas, even though they were clean. And her hair felt dry and unkempt, even though she had deep-conditioned it just that morning. The wealthy had that effect on her.

"I'm here to see Garreth Ungerstein," she said with some degree of authority. Who knew? Maybe the blond silhouette would think she was there to buy the club. Or give him an earful for serving cold chowder at the Fourth of July brunch. At the very least, maybe this way she wouldn't be treated like the trespassing nonmember she was.

"Garreth is lunching with the Lockharts," the blonde said, as if the event had been the lead story on *Regis and Kelly* that morning. "He should be done by two."

A moment of silence passed between them.

"You can wait over there if you'd like." She gestured toward a glossy wood end table wedged between two leather chairs. A crystal jar of peanuts and a fan arrangement of several golf magazines seemed anxious for company, like decorations at a party where no one showed up.

All of a sudden a loud splash reverberated in the distance, followed by a boom of coed laughter. The familiarity of the sound filled Kristen with comfort and cramps at the same time.

"Can I wait by the pool?"

The shadow considered this while tapping her black Montblanc pen on a thick, waterlogged reservations book. Computers must have given off too much light.

"Fine." She sighed lightly. "But no swimming. And stay off the green."

"Given," Kristen said with an eye roll and then hurried toward the heavy oak door, pushing it open before the receptionist changed her mind.

Outside, the bright sunlight was in sharp contrast to the dim foyer. The smoky gray lenses of Kristen's red Fossil sunglasses were useless—it felt like someone was throwing nail polish remover in her eyes. But when Kristen's pupils finally adjusted, things became a little too clear.

A cluster of shirtless boys in boldly patterned surf trunks was sharing green chaises with blondes in citrus-toned bikinis. Their chairs were pulled right up to the edge of the saltwater pool, and the girls' thin cover-ups lay drenched at their tanned feet. A tangle of headphone wires, fashion magazines, and half-eaten club sandwiches surrounded them like a fortress. And it was doing a great job at keeping the rest of the world on the other side. The scene looked like an ad from Roxy's old line, Foxy: *Why be a surfer when you can date one?*

Kristen watched it all unfold from across the pool, like an LBR who couldn't find a seat at the movies and was forced to stand at the back. She felt like her life was being lived without her. And if she didn't get it back soon, she'd die.

"Hey," Dune shout-waved at Kristen. He sat up and smiled, but Skye quickly pulled him back down onto her lap.

Kristen thought about pretending she hadn't heard him, but her legs overruled her brain. Next thing she knew, she had zigzagged through the forest of green deck chairs and was standing above them. "What's up?" she asked, as if they had been hanging poolside together for years.

"Heard Dune saved you last night," Skye said, tying a pink elastic around a tiny braid she'd made in the back of Dune's blond hair. She wore a lemon yellow string bikini with ruffles along the cleavage.

"At least someone did." Kristen smirked.

Skye lifted her blond brows in a did-you-*really*-just-talk-to-me-like-that sort of way.

"What's *that* supposed to mean?" asked Tyler, who was getting his cast decorated with napkin flowers by two of the DSL Daters. "If Skye hadn't shown up, we'd all be in juvie."

"Is *that* what you think happened?" Kristen glared at Ripple, who was crouched down by Jax's chaise, massaging his callused feet. "Because I have another theory." She glared at Ripple's cell phone, wondering if the text messages she'd more than likely sent to Skye were still on there.

"Let's stop talking about last night." Dune removed the braid.

"What are you doing here anyway? You're not a member," Skye whisper-announced just loud enough for everyone to hear. Ripple and the DSL Dater in a melon-colored bikini snickered.

"I have a meeting with the manager, Garreth Ungerstein." She lifted her nose in an eat-your-heart-out sort of way.

"Why? Are you gonna rat us out for last night?" Tyler lifted his cast at her in annoyance, sending three tissue flowers into the pool. Everyone watched helplessly as they sank.

"No!" Kristen snapped. Did they think she was *that* lame?

"Trying to join?" Skye smirked.

Kristen shrugged coyly. Why not let them think she could if she wanted to?

"I thought you hated this place," Dune whisper-insisted, sounding slightly disappointed.

"I thought *you* hated this place?" she whisper-hissed back, dodging Skye's question. At that moment, Kristen didn't care if she came off bitter or angry. He had sold his soul to Skye, Katie Holmes–style.

"We *did* hate this place . . . until we tried the pool," Tyler cut in. Just then Scooter floated by on a blow-up dolphin raft.

"And the clam sauce." Jax rubbed his finger along Ripple's back where DSL DATER IN TRAINING was written in red goo.

"Well, you guys can be my guests all summer if you want," Skye sighed. "It looks like I may not be going to Alphas."

"What? *Why?*" Kristen gasped, giving away just how much she'd been counting on the dancer sashaying out of Westchester for good.

Apparently too full of herself to realize that Kristen's reaction was one of disappointment, not sympathy, Skye took off her white frame Ray-Bans and lowered her blue eyes. "My application was lost in the mail. I could do it again and send it in, but that would mean writing another ten-page entrance essay on a winning attitude, and I'd rather spend the summer with"—she brushed her fingers along Dune's shoulder like she was checking for dust—"these guys."

"Awwwww." The DSL Daters dog-piled her for a group hug, taking Dune with them.

"Hey, let me in!" Jax jumped in.

"And meeee." Ripple dove on top of the heap.

In an effort to protect his arm, Tyler stood over the hug-fest and rested his butt on Ripple's back as if she were a giant beanbag.

Once again, Kristen stood to the side like an LBR and watched. "Don't you have the essay saved on your computer?" she tried.

"I had to handwrite it," Skye giggle-yelled from the bottom of the love pile. "They wanted to analyze our penmanship to gauge our personalities."

"Well, did you press hard with your pen?" Kristen tried again.

The group broke apart and Skye went through the motions of taming her wild curls. "What does *that* have to do with anything?"

"Sometimes, if you run a pencil over a pad of paper really softly, you can see what was written on the page before it." Kristen smile-shrugged like she was just trying to help. "It may be worth a try."

"The only thing worth a try are the club's virgin mango daiquiris!" Skye threw her arms in the air like she'd just jumped out of someone's birthday cake. "Who wants?"

"Meeeeee!" they all shouted.

Skye summoned the waiter by gracefully lifting her finger, the way a ballerina might complete a plié.

Kristen hid her tearing eyes by checking her Guess Carousel watch. "I better go. Garreth is probably waiting for me."

Skye shielded her eyes from the sun and looked out at the green. "Doesn't look like it." She tilted her head toward a tall man in white linen shorts and a green polo. He and a stout bald man wearing too much madras were getting into a cart, their clubs sticking out the back. "He probably won't be back for hours." She smirked.

Kristen felt like someone had shot a golf ball straight into her gut. "I'll just come back later," she managed. "I have tons to do today. See ya."

Without another word Kristen turned on her silver Pumas and bolted back to her mother's car, where she would begin a long afternoon of lying to Marsha about Garreth and all the wonderful things he'd said about her. And *that* would end up being the best part of her day.

Nothing is more pathetic than spending a beautiful summer day hiding out in bed when you're not:

A) Sick.
B) Jet-lagged.
C) Coming off an all-night study session.
D) Recovering from surgery.
E) All of the above. ✓

And Kristen was definitely E. She was depressed in a way that made Victoria Beckham look cheerful. Massie had been right from the very beginning. Dune was done. Skye had won. Seeing them together at the club had eliminated any last bits of hope she had been clinging to. And the only thing left to do now was cry about it.

Beep . . . beeeeep . . . beeeeeeeeeeeeeeeeeeeep.

David Beckham climbed up the side of Kristen's C-shaped body and licked her cheeks.

"I hear it. I hear it." She pushed the REPLY button on the left side of her watch, then stared up at the white ceiling, her body too heavy to do much more. Finally, with a groan,

Kristen sat and went through the necessary steps needed to get ready for her conference. But there was no joy in any of it. Suddenly, the Witty Committee felt like a goofy consolation prize, a second-place ribbon for those not pretty enough to win the crown.

Once she had been transformed into Cleopatra, Kristen powered up her screen and managed to turn on the charm. There were the familiar quadrants and four famous faces staring back at her through the LCD monitor.

EINSTEIN (Layne Abeley) **Disguise:** tweed coat, bushy mustache, wiry gray wig **Expertise:** physics	**BILL GATES (Danh Bondok)** **Disguise:** glasses, light blue button-down, dark blue blazer **Expertise:** technology
OPRAH (Rachel Walker) **Disguise:** wavy black wig, gold hoop earrings, pumpkin orange blouse **Expertise:** anthropology (the study of humankind, not the cute and affordable shabby-chic store)	**SHAKESPEARE (Aimee Snyder)** **Disguise:** gray bald-in-the-front, curly-in-the-back wig, mustache, white collar sticking out of a black cloak **Expertise:** affairs of the heart and the Romance languages

"What do we stand for?" Kristen asked like someone who cared.

"BOB," they answered.

"And what does BOB stand for?"

"Brains over beauty!"

"Whatevs," she muttered to herself with an eye roll so mini it was virtually undetectable. "What's going on?"

"We intercepted a text between Skye and Dune," Einstein panted in a way that suggested the task had required more from her than simply sitting in front of Danh's computer and watching him work.

"And?"

"*And* he's sneaking into the club tonight to go for a swim with Skye. After they made plans she texted the DSL Daters and told them they were going to lip-kiss."

Kristen lowered her head so her bangs would cover her moistening eyes. "It doesn't matter." She grinned. "It's over. I'm fine."

"*Yes!*" Bill Gates made a fist and squeezed.

"Bill!" Oprah huffed. "That's not very supportive."

"Wha'd I say?" He looked genuinely confused. "She said she's fine. I thought she was fine."

"A sad clown, at best." Shakespeare sighed despondently.

"I say you get out there and break them up," Einstein said with tremendous authority. "I think you two have some real chemistry."

"What do you know about love?" Kristen pouted.

"Um, does nineteen twenty-one mean anything to you?" Layne countered.

"You won the Nobel Prize in physics," Bill scoffed. "What does that have to do with *love*?"

"It proves I'm not an idiot."

Everyone giggled. Even Kristen.

"We also have proof that Ripple tipped Skye off the other night in exchange for a fast-track initiation into the DSL Daters," Bill Gates offered.

"I knew it!" The spark of Kristen's competitive nature returned. "She cheated!"

"Exactly!" Oprah smacked her own thigh. "And doesn't that just burn you up?"

"It does!" The molten lava stream of WC adoration flowed through her body once again. "What can I do?"

"We figured out a way for you to execute Dune's Jell-O prank," Einstein beamed.

"It took all night." Bill Gates removed his wire-frame glasses, rubbed his eyes, and put them back on. "And while I think you could do a lot better than this guy, I am anxious to see if we got the formula right. So I will acquiesce."

"I'm in!" Kristen hugged David Beckham until he meow-coughed.

"Stand by, people," Oprah bellowed. "By midnight we'll know if he's the yang to your yin."

"Or if you're star-crossed lovers," Shakespeare added.

"Or if Love $= K\&D^2$."

"Or if we can chill seventeen thousand gallons of Jell-O on a hot summer night," Bill Gates guffawed.

Their enthusiasm was infectious, and hope returned to Kristen like a loyal puppy. And that made her feel beautiful. Even if Dune was too Skye-struck to notice.

Dressed as their favorite Gifteds, Kristen (Cleopatra), Aimee (Shakespeare), and Rachel (Oprah) were breaking down three hundred empty Jell-O boxes, trying not to complain about the paper cuts, leg cramps, and mosquito bites they were getting from crouch-hiding. They had been behind the shrubs that surrounded the pool area for three hours, while Einstein and Bill Gates tinkered with wires and homemade refrigeration mechanisms, in a nail-biting race against time to chill the strawberry flavor-crystals before Skye and Dune arrived for their midnight swim.

Kristen's watch beeped after the guards made their ninth security pass. "It's time," she whisper-announced.

Oprah and Shakespeare nodded. Without a word they made a mad, barefoot dash across the golf course, each with a lemon yellow pillowcase (Martha Stewart Collection) stuffed full of empty Jell-O boxes. Their plan was to bury them in the sand traps on the golf course, then make an anonymous call in the morning so they could be dug up and recycled. And they pulled it off in record time. After a quick burial, they were back behind the bushes, silent-high-five-giggle-panting at the success of their mission.

Kristen's forehead was sweating under her wig. Her hands were clammy. And her mouth was dry. Not so much because of the humidity, but because this scheme was by far the most ambitious one she had ever been a part of—Pretty Committee included. And while failure would mean going back to the drawing board for her accomplices, for Kristen it would mean game over. No Dune. No fun. No reason to get out of bed until September.

"Ready!" Bill Gates whisper-announced while Layne scurried around the deck collecting blue Post-its filled with schematics and formulas that had dropped out of Bill's overflowing code binder.

Kristen sigh-peered through the dense leaves, fighting her urge to call the whole thing off. Yes, it was an incredible accomplishment—speed-chilling Jell-O on an eighty-degree night—but beyond that, their plan would never work: Skye would *never* jump into the oversize strawberry-flavored Jell-O bowl and become too goopy to lip-kiss Dune. As soon as she arrived, she'd see the gigantic pink gelatinous slab where seventeen thousand gallons of water used to be. Dune would arrive, and then they'd have a big laugh about it, falling into each other's arms. Then Skye would take credit for the whole thing and Dune would give up surfing to spend his days drifting in her sea blue eyes.

"We're almost set." Bill Gates licked his lips hungrily and opened his silver MacBook Air. "I need room—can everyone *please* give me some room?"

Oprah, Shakespeare, and Cleopatra did a three-step reverse crouch-walk, like sumo wrestlers in rewind.

Einstein pulled a Tupperware container of blue water and a slim flashlight from the inside pocket of her tweed blazer. "Ready?"

Bill Gates nodded.

She lifted the lid, shook the water ever so slightly, and shone her light on it. Bill Gates captured the image with his computer's camera and somehow managed to send it to a projector he had perched atop the snack bar roof. With a few quick right clicks, the image was sent to the pool.

Kristen gasped, then quickly covered her open mouth with her sweat-drenched palm. The pool suddenly appeared to be full of gentle lapping water.

Oprah and Shakespeare drew back their breath in awe.

"Where there's a will, there's a wave." Bill Gates grin-winked at Layne.

She grin-winked back.

"You're geniuses!" Kristen hugged them like two giant stuffed animals. At that moment, dressed in a Grecian gown and black bob wig, surrounded by Bill Gates, Einstein, Oprah, and Shakespeare, Kristen had never been more proud to be a part of anything in her life. Not the OCD soccer team, not the competitive scholarship program, not the Sudoku Society, not Students for BO (Barack Obama)—not even the Pretty Committee.

"Shhhhhhhhh." Oprah pulled them apart. "Look." She whisper-pointed at the lithe figure wearing a white string bikini, tangles of gold scarves, and a straw cowboy hat. Skye looked around (for Dune? A security guard?), and when she saw that no one was there, she pulled out her phone and answered a text.

Bill quickly shuttled to another screen on his computer and intercepted.

DSL1: Is he there?
Skye: ☹
DSL1: U gonna wait?
Skye: Few minutes.
DSL1: Bikini?

Skye held out her phone, snapped a quick shot of her torso, and forwarded it.

DSL1: Luv it! Hope the white's not see-thru.
Skye: Hope it is. ☺

Kristen gasped. If *this* was her competition, she didn't stand a chance.

When DSL1 didn't respond, Kristen pointed to her screen name, then herself. Bill Gates immediately understood her question and nodded yes.

Kristin slid beside him and he angled the silver keypad toward herself. She giggle-typed as her gifted contemporaries looked on in wonder and amusement.

DSL1: Jump in and find out. So sexy if you're already in the pool.

Skye: Nah. Got my own plan, thx.

With that, Skye threw her phone on a chaise and Kristen's shoulders rolled forward in defeat. But they didn't stay that way for long. Skye, the ultimate alpha, had rejected her friend's advice only because she hadn't thought of it herself.

But that didn't mean she wasn't going to take it.

After another check for security, she pulled off her scarves, tossed them over her shoulder, and walked straight for the pool.

Oprah grabbed Shakespeare's hand. Shakespeare grabbed Einstein's. Einstein grabbed Kristen's. Kristen grabbed Bill's. And Bill smiled.

They lowered their chins and bit their lips, doing whatever they could to keep from laughing out loud.

When she got to the edge of the deep end, Skye hooked her finger around the back of her bikini bottom and pulled the creeping material from her butt crack. *Now* she was ready . . . but she didn't move. Instead she stood perfectly still, her pink pedicured toes curled over the concrete and her arms pressed against her sides.

"What is she doing?" mouthed Einstein.

Everyone shrugged.

Flip-flop . . . flip-flop . . . flip-flop . . .

Suddenly they heard what she heard. Dune was getting

closer. And, like Massie always said, why take the stage during intermission? In other words, if no one is watching, why bother doing?

"Hey," Dune whisper-greeted Skye as he got closer.

Skye pretended she didn't know he was there and jumped.

She bent at the knees (showing off her chiseled dancer's legs), lifted her arms over her head (like she was the Sugar Plum Fairy in the Nutcracker), and pushed off with her toes.

Kristen held her breath and squeezed her eyes shut.

Next came the sound of someone slapping a fat man's gut, followed by the muted shriek of a girl who'd landed headfirst in chilly, jiggling, NutraSweetened Jell-O. Kristen opened one eye. Then another. Bill Gates had shut off the water reflection, and Skye now looked like a mini marshmallow in vat of pink Jell-O. The Witty Committee broke out in laughter.

Flip-flop flip-flop flip-flop flip-flop flip-flop flip-flop . . .

Dune hurried to her rescue.

When he got to the edge and saw the blonde covered in wiggly red chunks, he burst out laughing. "What a sucker punch!"

Kristen picked at her cuticles, unsure whether his laughter would:

A) Bring them closer

B) Drive them apart.

C) Alert Dwight the security guard and get them all arrested.

"Get me out of here!" Skye slapped her arms down. The entire pink pool trembled.

Yes! It was B!

"Is this your idea of a practical joke?" She pulled a red chunk off her clavicle and whipped it at his ah-dorable stomach. It landed with a smack, then fell to the deck with a lifeless thud, making him laugh even harder.

Kristen fought the urge to run out and throw her arms around his giggle-quaking shoulders.

"How am I going to return this bathing suit now?" Skye moaned while Dune pulled her out. "You did this, didn't you? You and your *jealous* wannabe-member friends."

"Actually, *you* look like the *Jell*-Os one," he joked.

The Witty Committee exchanged enthusiastic high fives on his behalf.

Skye searched his face angrily. Had he really just spoken to her like that?

But his amused smile refused to back down. In fact, the more she huffed, the wider it got.

"Ugh!" She grabbed her phone and scarves and marched off into the darkness.

"Skye, wait!" Dune called after her. Yet he stood still.

Kristen's insides were pushing against her skin, urging her forward, unable to stand one more second in hiding.

She'd fought hard.

She'd fought smart.

And now she wanted her prize.

"Here." Oprah handed her a clear orange Juicy beach tote. Inside was a can of whipped cream and two spoons. "It's fat-free." She winked.

Looking out at her betas, Kristen's eyes filled with happy tears. She wanted to make a speech to show them how grateful she was for their brilliance and support, but she didn't have a chance. In one swift movement, Einstein pulled off her Cleopatra wig and Shakespeare playfully shoved her out of the bushes. Intermission was over. And they were dying to see how this love story would end.

Kristen would have liked a moment to collect her thoughts. Or rehearse her opening line. Or gloss. But Dune noticed her the instant she flew out of the shrubs.

"What are you doing here?" He lifted his head and lowered his phone mid-text.

"Sweet tooth." She held-swung the bag of whipped cream as she flip-flopped toward him, suddenly aware of the silky white Grecian dress against her illegally shaved legs. That, and the way he was beaming, reassured Kristen that gloss wasn't necessary. With the Witty Committee behind her, the warm summer breeze around her, and Dune smile-waiting for her just ahead, Kristen felt perfect just the way she was.

"Did you do all this?" Dune's light brown eyes looked like they had been sprinkled with glitter.

"I had a little help." She casually put her hand behind her back and flashed a thumbs-up to the Witty Committee.

"How'd ya know I'd be here?" Dune asked, with the amused confusion of someone who had just walked into his own surprise party. "How did you pull it off? Why did you do it?"

Finally, a question she wanted to answer.

"I thought we were going to get revenge. And when I saw you at the pool today, I figured you were casing it, you know, so we could do this," she lied. "I didn't realize you were into Skye. I didn't think she was your type." She let her voice trail off like a seasoned soap actress. "Sorry if I ruined things between you guys," she lied again.

"You didn't." Dune took the bag out of Kristen's hand and pulled out the whipped cream. "The whole reason I came by tonight was to tell her I only wanted to be friends." He pulled the red top off the can of Reddi-wip. "And now I'm not sure I even want that. That OCDiva can't take a sucker punch. How lame!"

"Yeah, I guess you must have met, like, a million pretty girls on your surf trips you'd rather hang with." Kristen widened her eyes, trying to look cheery about it.

"Yeah." He got down on one knee and began drawing a whipped cream heart on the pool deck. "But none of them have it all." He paused. "Like you."

A muted mini *awwww* whined out from the bushes behind them.

Suddenly, Kristen's insides felt like they had been filled with helium. And if she didn't grab hold of something soon, she'd float up into the starry sky and never see him again.

"What do you think?" Dune stood and waved his tanned arm over his masterpiece. Inside the heart he had written KG & DB.

The whipped cream would probably melt in less than an hour, but the memory would last forever.

"I see them!" shouted a man's voice from somewhere in the darkness. "Freeze!"

It was Dwight.

Panic instantly chased the floaty feeling from Kristen's body. Her heart was no longer thumping to the beat of love ballads. It was more like the theme from the TV show *Cops—Bad boys, bad boys whatchu gonna do / whatchu gonna do when they come for you.* . . .

"Come on!" Dune grabbed Kristen's arm and pulled her under a chaise. They lay side by side on the warm deck, panting and squeezing each other's hands. If she hadn't been at risk of being punished for an entire year, this would have been the best moment of her life.

Suddenly, a static-soaked voice bleated out over a walkie-talkie, "Three suspects just ran from the bushes but one is still there gathering up some computer gear."

"Can you get a positive ID?" Dwight asked.

"Um, well, it kind of looks like Albert Einstein." The other guard chuckled.

"Layne!" Kristen mouthed to Dune.

"This is no time for jokes, Karl. Apprehend! I'll head over to the fence and nab the others before they crawl under. Maybe *now* Garreth will take my security memos more seriously." He huffed as he took off toward the green.

"Come on." Kristen began wiggling out from under the chaise. "Now's our chance!"

She took off toward the main entrance of the club. With the guards running in the opposite direction, it was the perfect place to slip out.

"Where are you going?" Dune whisper-shouted.

Kristen stopped and looked back. He was heading toward the bushes, straight for Karl.

"That's the wrong way," she insisted. Then mouthed, "Karl."

"Don't you want to save your friend?" he asked, his body still turned toward the bushes.

"I can't! I'll be grounded for a year if I get caught." As she said the words, her eyes filled with tears. Getting caught meant no Dune, no sleepovers at Massie's, and no soccer until the ninth grade! The stakes were too high. Even for a member of the Witty Committee.

"You can't leave a buddy behind!"

"I won't be able to see you until next summer." She squeezed the billowing material of her dress with suddenly sweat-slicked palms.

Dune studied her face as if he had just woken from a

coma. "You're not going to see me anyway." He quickly turned and raced toward Layne.

But it was too late.

"Ahhhhhhh!" she shouted as Karl crept up behind her and blinded her with his industrial-size flashlight.

Tears began rolling down Kristen's cheeks as she struggled to decide between:

A) Saving her friend.
B) Saving her relationship.
C) Saving herself.

Her head chose A. Her heart chose B. But her legs chose C.

Kristen pulled her phone from the pocket of her white cotton dress and stared at its screen.

The envelope icon on her black Razr wasn't there, just like it hadn't been there the last eight times she'd checked.

Each time Kristen thought about last night she kicked her soccer ball as hard as she could. And each time, it slammed against the cement wall that surrounded the roof of her building with a *thwack*.

How could she have left Layne behind?

Thwack!

How could Dune have left *her* behind?

Thwack!

Would she rather be punished for a year and have Dune's respect?

Thwack!

Or have freedom and no one to share it with?

Thwack!

The sun was bearing down on her unprotected scalp like a judgmental eye. And the deserted black tar roof offered no relief. In fact, it felt like she was burning in a concrete hell, and, certain she deserved it, Kristen chose to stick it out.

Technically, with no job, no friends, and no crush, hell was everywhere she went, but up here, no one could see her cry . . . or sweat—two things she had been doing all morning.

Finally, Kristen allowed herself a long sip of tap water from her Evian bottle. She wiped her mouth on her salty arm, then pulled her black Razr from the pocket on her white H&M cargo dress (which would accidentally get caught on a nail and be ripped to shreds one week before the Pretty Committee got back).

No messages.

Thwack!

She shuffled across the scorching tar to retrieve her ball but stopped midway when her cell vibrated. It was a text.

From . . . *Dune*!

Dune: Need to talk ASAP. Where are you?
Kristen: Roof. Pinewood bldg. Take elevator to ninth floor.
Dune: See u in three minutes.

Three minutes?
Thwack!

Kristen tried to catch a glimpse of her reflection in the bottom of an abandoned Budweiser can, but hot beer trickled out all over her arm and made her chive-scented BO smell even worse. She ran around the perimeter of the roof, looking for a faucet, but found nothing. Maybe she could text Dune back and tell him to come over in an hour. After she had some time to shower and rehearse her this-is-why-I-left-a-buddy-behind speech.

But it was too late.

A car door slammed below, and, sure enough, Brice's blue Chevy Avalanche pulled away.

There would be no shower.

Thwack!

No gloss.

Thwack!

No rehearsal.

Thwack!

No—

The metal door to the roof opened suddenly with a pump-hiss.

Kristen dried her eyes, then turned slowly, as if weighed down by shame.

A stocky blond with frizzy hair and brown terry cloth jumper stood before her fanning her face. "I bet you could get a killer tan up here," the girl said. "It's much closer to the sun than my roof. You can feel it."

"Ripple?" Kristen's heart sank like the elevator she wished she was taking her back down to her condo.

"Yeah, sorry." She shrugged. "I pulled Dune's phone out of his pocket just before Dad dropped him off at GAS."

"Why?"

"If you got a text from me, would you have responded?"

She lifted her face to the sun-soaked sky.

Kristen didn't have to say a word. They both knew the answer.

"What do you want?" she asked, kicking the black-and-white ball. It rebounded off the wall and landed right back at her cleats. A move she wished Dune had been there to see.

Ripple pulled a black elastic off her wrist and tied back her perma-parched hair. "Turns out Skye got accepted to Alphas after all."

For an instant, Kristen felt lighter than Kate Bosworth. Then she realized Skye's absence wouldn't bring her any closer to Dune. That was so yesterday. So before-he-saw-her-turn-her-back-on-Layne. "And?"

"*And* she's being all *un* toward the DSL Daters." Ripple kicked a cigarette butt with her clear jellies. "She's dismantling the group. Says she only wants to hang with dancers now."

"*And?*"

"*Annnnnndddd* I want you to be my tutor again so I can get Massie-fied. I'm offering you your old job back. You'll get to see *Duuuu-uuuuune*."

The heat on the roof suddenly seemed unbearable.

"Forget the job." Kristen lifted her hair and fanned he back of her neck. "I'll tell you what you need to know for free."

Ripple speed-nodded and air-clapped. "I'm ready." Her

mouth hung open, ready to gobble up whatever Kristen had to offer.

"Massie thinks wannabes are LBRs minus ten."

Ripple crinkled her brows in confusion.

"If she thinks you're trying to be like her, she won't like you. She only likes people who like themselves. And she only respects people who like themselves more than they like her. You have to accept who you are and own it. So if you're living your life to impress other people, which is what *you're* doing—"

"And what *you're* doing," Ripple snapped.

Ouch!

Her accusation hit Kristen like a much-needed bucket of ice water. For a dumb nine-year-old, Ripple was kind of smart.

"Correction—it's what I *was* doing." Kristen jammed her toe under her soccer ball, flipped it up, and caught it. "Those days are over. Class dismissed."

"THE COMMITTEE IS ASSEMBLED," announced the computer-generated voice.

Kristen sat at her white IKEA desk and lowered her eyes, unable to face what she had done, or the people she had done it to.

EINSTEIN (Layne Abeley)

Disguise: tweed coat, bushy mustache, wiry gray wig

Expertise: physics

BILL GATES (Danh Bondok)

Disguise: glasses, light blue button-down, dark blue blazer

Expertise: technology

OPRAH (Rachel Walker)

Disguise: wavy black wig, gold hoop earrings, pumpkin orange blouse

Expertise: anthropology (the study of humankind, not the cute and affordable shabby-chic store)

SHAKESPEARE (Aimee Snyder)

Disguise: gray bald-in-the-front, curly-in-the-back wig, mustache, white collar sticking out of a black cloak

Expertise: affairs of the heart and the Romance languages

"What do we stand for?" she asked under the cover of her Cleopatra wig.

"BOB," they answered.

"And what does BOB stand for?"

"Brains over beauty!"

Kristen sighed and then decided to just say it. "I am officially resigning as the leader of the Witty Committee," she told the grass-stained hem of her white silk goddess dress.

"What? Why?" Bill Gates screeched. His unconstrained passion forced Kristen to lift her eyes. "We thought you called the meeting to thank us."

"Well, that too." Kristen felt like she had one of David Beckham's fur balls in the back of her throat. "What you did for me last night was—"

"Not last night, girl." Oprah shook her head. *"Today."*

"What are you talking about?"

"Skye got her acceptance letter to Alphas this morning, didn't you hear?" Shakespeare smirked. "And I am pleased to say I wrote her entire essay with a quill."

Einstein, Oprah, and Bill applauded.

Kristen grinned but wasn't exactly sure why. "What did you do?"

"I got rid of her for good." Shakespeare smiled. "Heaven knows I was no help when it came to last night's tech circus. So I contributed in my own way and wrote a brilliant essay in iambic pentameter."

"Seriously?" Kristen grabbed the sides of the screen and kissed it like it was Aimee's face. "I thought you guys were mad at me."

"We were," Layne said, using her best German Einstein accent. "But after the Witty Committee rescued me from the country club cops, we thought about all the stupid things we did when we were in crush mode. And we decided to forgive you."

"Like what?" Kristen giggled in anticipation.

"You know the hole I drilled in the pipes at Briarwood?" Layne smiled sheepishly. "The one that caused the wave pool to leak and destroy the whole facility?"

Kristen speed-nodded. She had no idea where this was going, but she certainly remembered getting the news before summer break that the boys' school had collapsed and was submerged underwater.

"Well, I did it because I wanted my crush, Dempsey, to go to OCD." Her cheeks turned bright red. Surrounded by the silver wig, she looked like a Christmas tree ornament draped in tinsel.

"No *way*!" Kristen covered her mouth in shock. "How did you know it would work?"

"The OCD manifest states that in the case of emergency, one school will take in the other." Layne shrugged. "It was a no-brainer. He gets back from Bali mid-September. I can't wait to tell him the news. I've already reserved a locker for him next to mine."

Kristen's hand was still on her mouth as she shook her head in utter disbelief.

"And I intercepted Skye's first essay so she'd stay in Westchester." Bill Gates dabbed his forehead with a screen-cleaning cloth.

"Since when do you like *Skye*?" Kristen squealed, feeling one percent jealous. Even though she didn't like Danh in *that* way, she liked that he liked her. And she loved that he liked her more than Skye.

"I don't." Bill's neck was starting to break out in red blotches.

"*Tell* her," Oprah gently nudged.

"I like *you*," he blurted. "I was hoping she'd stay here, Dune would stay with her, and you'd be free."

"*Awwww*, Bill." Kristen touched her heart. "I'm so, so—"

"It's okay." Bill smiled like he meant it. "I'm moving on."

"You see," Shakespeare spoke up, "I agreed to wear this stupid costume and write with a feather because I like Bill." She looked up, so it appeared she was making love-eyes at Bill on Kristen's screen. Bill glanced down at her quadrant and smiled.

The two giggled as if they had already made it official with a lip kiss or two.

"Don't you just love all this honesty?" Oprah gushed.

"So you forgive me?" Kristen asked everyone, but mostly Layne.

"If you promise one thing." Layne tucked a wiry gray

wig strand behind her ear. "Help me get Dempsey next year before someone else snatches him up."

"I swear." Kristen lifted her pinky, knowing Dempsey was a total LBR. The blond, green-eyed chubby gamer who worked the lighting board for the Young Actors' Program at the community playhouse would be lucky times ten to land a girl like Layne.

"Then you're forgiven." She lifted her pinky and touched it to the camera on her computer. For a second, her quadrant was filled with an oversize pink finger.

"What are *you* going to do?" Shakespeare asked.

Kristen's happy bubble popped as her thoughts were forced back to Dune. She had no idea what she was going to do. No idea how to live with this sadness for the rest of the summer. No idea how to convince him to give her a second chance.

"Knock, knock," a boy's voice said from her bedroom doorway. "Can I come in?"

She was about to find out.

"What are you doing here?" Kristen quickly closed her MacBook, pulled the Cleopatra wig off her head, and jammed it under her green and blue duvet. Her sweat-drenched hair had dried into what probably looked like Donald Trump in a windstorm. And she was wearing the same Greek goddess dress he'd seen her in last night. But she would never compromise the Witty Committee for love again, not even when her looks were at stake. So she grabbed her mint green satin VS robe off the floor and casually slipped it on to avoid questions.

"I came to say goodbye." Dune hooked his thumbs under the straps of his red Gravis backpack.

Kristen's stomach pitched. Hope was gone.

"I thought you already said goodbye at the country club," she said coolly. Inside her mind, a soccer stadium–size crowd jumped out of their seats and cheered for her quick retort and iron resolve.

Dune lowered his black fedora, then stuffed his hands in the pockets of his khaki cargo shorts. A tattered white beater showed off his defined, tanned shoulders, which happened to be slumped forward in shame. "Yeah, about that . . ."

"Whatevs." Kristen twirled her finger around her locket,

channeling Massie and her strength. "So, where are you going?"

Despite the somber moment, he couldn't help smiling. "Tavarua. It's an island in Fiji. Totally exclusive, with one of the best breaks in the world."

"Is this because of *last night*?"

Dune chuckled. He dropped his bag on the floor and hurried over. Unsure of what to do when a CLAM got that close to her and her bed, Kristen slid onto her blue shag area rug, her back resting against a green and white sham. He immediately sat down beside her, smelling like coconuts and sunshine.

"Nah. Earlier this summer I booked a commercial for Billabong." He beamed. "We shoot on the island for a week, and then Dad, Ripple, and I are going to camp on the beach and surf until my tour starts."

"Good luck." Kristen stood.

"Wait." He pulled her back down.

The warmth of his hand melted the ice behind her eyes. Tears were imminent and only a matter of time. Kristen glanced toward her window as if something life altering was about to happen beyond the pane.

"I thought maybe you could tell me how you did the whole Jell-O thing. It'll go over huge with the guys on tour."

She pulled her hand away. "*That's* why you came?"

Dune blinked several times, as if his lashes were slapping his face for saying something so stupid.

And then he shook his head no.

"Then why are you here?" Kristen's voice shook. She wasn't sure if she was offended, heartbroken, or angry. All she knew was that Dune looked like he was gearing up to say something worth e-mailing to her friends, and she could hardly wait a second longer. "Tell me!"

He looked up, his eyes a darker shade of brown than she remembered. "I came to tell you I'm sorry I left you last night. And that I'm sorry I'm leaving you this summer. And that I'm sorry I didn't have a chance to get to know you better."

David Beckham jumped onto Dune's lap and purred for both of them.

Kristen ran a hand through her matted hair and smiled in a way that told him all was forgiven. "What do you want to know?"

"I want to know who you *are*." He shifted to face her.

Kristen giggled at his question. It sounded like a stolen line from one of those corny Lifetime movies her mother watched. But his expression remained fixed and she knew he meant it.

And that was one of the many things she ah-dored about him.

"I'm a lot of things, I guess." She tied the green satin tie on her robe in mini knots while she contemplated.

With the Pretty Committee she was:

A) Popular times ten.
B) Stylish.

C) Snobby.

D) Smarter then the rest of them, but not as smart as she really was.

E) A soccer star.

F) Waxed.

G) Fake-rich.

H) A beta.

I) Insecure.

F) Loyal.

H) All of the above. ✓

With the Witty Committee she was:

A) An alpha.

B) Intellectually gifted.

C) An LBR lover.

D) CC (Closet Cleopatra).

E) Loyal.

F) Proud.

G) Confident.

H) All of the above. ✓

With her mother she was:

A) Studious.

B) Obedient.

C) Modest.

D) Frumpy.

E) Middle class.

F) Proud.

G) Independent.

H) A future president.

I) Hairy-legged.

J) All of the above. ✓

The truth was, Kristen Gregory was so many things, she had no idea how to answer his question.

"I dunno," was all she could manage.

Dune lifted his arms and reached behind his head. "Why don't you think about it while I'm gone." He unhooked his leather-tied shark tooth necklace, leaned forward, and fastened it around her neck.

"What are you doing?" she asked, praying her question wouldn't change his mind. "Isn't this important to you?"

"It is." He grinned. "That's why you better be here when I get back in October."

"October?" Kristen gasped.

"Everything okay in here?" Marsha poked her head inside the open doorway. Kristen quickly shimmied away from Dune.

"Yeah, why?" Her cheeks burned.

"I thought I heard you calling for me," Marsha said convincingly, even though they all knew she was lying.

"Nope, wasn't me." Kristen glared at her.

"Ooops, sorry." Marsha turned, "accidentally" elbow-knocking the door open a little bit more.

Kristen eye-rolled an apology on her mother's behalf. Dune smirked that he understood.

Then she lifted her hand and clutched the necklace just to make sure this was really happening. The worn leather . . . the smooth surface of the tooth . . . the sharp tip. The different textures felt so rugged against the smooth contours of her Coach locket and its delicate gold chain. It was clear just from holding them that the two pendants were never intended to be worn together—something Massie would inevitably point out. One was so elegant and pristine, while the other was gritty and real. Yet she understood them both. But she knew that once school started, when style mattered more than substance, one of them would have to go.

Dune stood. "I better jet. Dad's waiting for me outside."

Kristen stood too, waves of sadness, relief, and excitement crashing inside her like the perfect storm.

"I can't wait to see you when I get back." Dune looked toward the open door, thought for a second, then pulled her in for a hug.

"Me too." She hugged him back, wondering which Kristen Gregory would be there to greet him when he returned.

Now that you know Kristen's summer secret,
you're another step closer to being **IN**.
In the know, that is. . . .

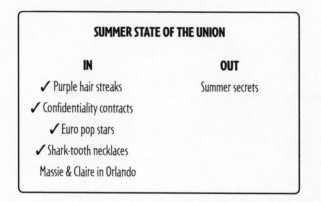

SUMMER STATE OF THE UNION

IN	**OUT**
✓ Purple hair streaks	Summer secrets
✓ Confidentiality contracts	
✓ Euro pop stars	
✓ Shark-tooth necklaces	
Massie & Claire in Orlando	

Five girls. Five stories. One ah-mazing summer.

THE CLIQUE
SUMMER COLLECTION

BY LISI HARRISON

*Turn the page for a sneak peek
of Claire's story. . . .*

"Hey, sweetheaaaa't, can ya move a little faster? Mrs. Wilkes wants her plants watered by three and she's seven blocks away." Todd Lyons stretched out on the yellow terry cloth–covered chaise and folded his hands behind his head. his DON'TCHA WISH YOUR BOYFRIEND WAS HOT LIKE ME? T-shirt lay in a heap on the deck, and a swim coach's whistle necklace dangled above his gray, shark-covered swim trunks.

"I can't go to Mrs. Wilkes's." Claire skimmed the surface of the drowned bug–infested pool with a net. "I told you that last week." She wiped her beading forehead with the back of her hand, then dried it on her turquoise Gap drawstring shorts, her gray tank already too sweaty and no longer an option.

"I'll have to dock your pay." Todd unscrewed the top off a tube of zinc oxide and smeared the thick white cream all over his freckly cheeks. Combined with his shock of over-grown red hair and the yellow chaise, the sunblock made him look like a ten-year-old Ronald McDonald. But as a boss he was more like Jerk-in-the-Box.

"Whatevs." Claire skimmed the pool one last time, then dropped the long pole. It fell to the cement deck with a resounding clang. If she was going to be docked, why not leave now? That way she could shower before her long-awaited reunion with her FBFF (Florida BFF) and style her hair with the cute flips on the bottom, the way Massie had taught her.

Puuuuurp!

Todd blew his whistle. "Watch the attitude," he warned, his eyes closed and lifted to the sun. "And don't forget, Piper is booked for a walk and shampoo tomorrow morning at eight."

"I know." Claire pulled the bobby pin out of her hair and shook her long bangs loose. It was times like these she wondered if working for her brother was worth it. But her goal was to earn enough money for a Massie-approved back-to-school wardrobe—or at least a cool pair of jeans—and so far, Todd was the only person in town willing to hire a twelve-year-old.

Maybe now that Sarah, Sari, and Mandy were finally back from sleepover camp, working for T-Odd Jobs, Inc., would stop sucking so much. Not that car washing, gardening, pool cleaning, dog walking, and bird sitting would suddenly become fun. Or that depending on her brother for a paycheck would become less pathetic. Or that doing all the work while he barked orders from the sidelines would become less humiliating. But with the girls around, life off the clock would be filled with side-splitting laughter, DIY crafts, and sugary snacks. And it was about time. Claire had waited all summer for summer to start. And with only four weeks left before her parents sold the house and moved everyone back to Westchester, she didn't want to waste another second.

Pedaling down Cherry Street on her old black and pink turbo Powerpuff Girls bike, Claire breathed in the citrus-scented air. She had missed the palm trees and orange trees over the last year. She had craved the thick, hot air that warmed her like one of Massie's old pashminas. And she loved making a wish every time a speedy little lizard zipped past her bare feet. As much as she'd grown to appreciate life in Westchester, Kissimmee was still home. And with the return of Sarah, Sari, and Mandy, it would finally start feeling like it.

Claire turned up the driveway of her soon to be ex–sky blue split-level ranch house, where three Razor scooters were lying on the grassy lawn beside the SOLD sign.

"Ehmagosh!" She jumped off her bike. It slammed to the ground, wheels still spinning.

"Ahhhhhh," shouted three girls from Claire's open bedroom window.

"Ahhhhh," Claire shouted back as she threw open the front door, bolted by her father, and took the peach carpeted stairs two at a time. "You're early!" she called, silently telling herself not to worry about her toxic pits and limp hair. It wasn't the Pretty Committee on the other side of her Hello Kitty sticker–covered door. These were her down-to-earth, wear-the-same-pair-of-socks-three-days-in-a-row *sisters*. She'd never cared about her looks before. . . .

After a quick extra-spitty lip lick (poor-girl's gloss) and a speedy cheek pinch (PG's blush), Claire barged into her lemon yellow bedroom, her bare feet sinking into the green shag carpet.

"CLAIRE-BEAR!" The girls rushed toward her for a group hug, but Claire kept her arms pinned to her sides. It was either that or get nicknamed Bad Pitt by Massie, should word somehow get back to New York.

"Where's the love?" Mandy pulled away, her thick black eyebrows more noticeable than they had been a year ago. "You're so s-t-i-f-f."

"Is that a Westchester thang?" Sari smiled, her thin upper lip disappearing against her slightly buck teeth.

"Or a New York tr-eeeend?" Sarah shimmied a like a limbo dancer preparing to slip under the pole.

Claire smiled warmly. Mandy still spelled! Sari still said "thang"! And Sarah was still in-sane! Like an old song that brings back memories of a long-forgotten crush, these quirky traits brought Claire back to that place she was just before she moved. A place where gloss was saved for class photos, blush was for Halloween, and body odor was perfectly natural.

"None of the above. I just have a little BO." Claire giggled.

"More like MO." Mandy lifted her long, thin arm and

pointed at Claire's daisy fabric–covered twin headboard. The cheery white and green floral print had been poked with pushpins that held dozens of Pretty Committee photos. Shots of the girls lying on sleeping bags, piling in the back of the Range Rover, cheering at soccer games, carving the Chanel logo out of snow, dangling tuna sashimi from their mouths, latte-toasting at Sixbucks, flying the Gelding Studios private jet to Hollywood, and several silly fashion poses with the Massie-quin were all on display.

"What's MO?" Claire asked, half smiling, half fearing the answer.

"Moved On." Mandy pouted.

Claire's white-blond eyelashes fluttered in confusion.

"Or Massie Obsession," Sari twirled her long blond hair, something she always did when goading someone.

"Or Meeee-Owwww," Claire purred like Catwoman, desperate to put an end to their teasing. Not because she couldn't take it, but because it forced her to consider the truth behind it. Which she was not ready to do. Wasn't it possible to like both sets of friends equally?

"Or Making Out!" Sarah lifted the one photo that was facing backward, kissed it, and then buried it in her mess of short, dirty blond curls. But Claire still managed to catch a forbidden glimpse of her ex-crush Cam Fisher winking his green eye.

At the beginning of the summer, when she'd hung the picture, Claire had made a pact with herself not to look at it until Cam responded to one of the many I'm-sorry-for-spy-ing-on-you-through-the-secret-camera-that-was-planted-in-your-sensitivity-training-class-and-I-will-never-do-anything-like-that-again-if-you-give-me-a-second-chance letters she sent him at summer camp. Which he hadn't yet done. And seeing him now, even for a second, conjured the rich, woodsy smell of his Drakkar Noir cologne and the heaviness that came with missing him. The sudden sensation was dizzying. Claire lowered herself onto the edge of her bed and sighed, leaking joy like a punctured balloon.

Sari gently sat down beside her, covering her bony knees with her pink TJ Maxx sundress. "We're only kidding, Claire-Bear," she said in her usual plugged-up nasally voice, the voice that usually made Claire giggle. She held out a Ziploc bag of candy corn.

Claire shook her head no.

"T-r-u-e." Mandy sat too, her sea foam green gauze pants scratching the side of Claire's thigh. "We just missed you. And these pictures prove you forgot about us."

"I didn't!" Claire insisted. "You should see my computer. You're my screen saver *and* my wallpaper."

Sarah pulled the picture of Cam out of her hair and pinned it back to the headboard, facing forward this time. "Thank gosh *Dial L for Loser* was a flop, or we would have lost you forever!"

"Opposite of true!" Claire blurted, stealing one of Alicia's lines.

"Whaddaya mean?" Sari play-smacked Claire's arm. "It tanked."

Claire burst out laughing. "I mean the part about losing me was opposite of true. I *know* the movie tanked."

They all cracked up a little more than necessary. And Claire couldn't help wondering if, like her, it was a way to release the stress that had been building up inside each one of them over the last year. Stress that came from constantly wondering if your best friend had found someone better.

But as they slapped the daisy-covered bed and wiped the giggle-tears from their eyes, the answer was obvious. They were back in a groove. And things would stay that way as long as Claire could show them that Massie and the Pretty Committee hadn't changed her a bit. Which wouldn't be *too* hard . . . right?

THE CLIQUE
SUMMER COLLECTION
BY LISI HARRISON

CLAIRE 8/5/2008

BATTLE OF THE BFFS!

Back in Orlando for the summer, Claire is reunited with her Florida best friends after a long year apart. Her FBFFs haven't changed at all. Too bad they think Claire has . . . and not for the better. And when a very special visitor shows up, Claire finds herself torn between Keds and couture. Will Claire finally kiss-immee her past goodbye — once and for all?

poppy
www.pickapoppy.com
Available Wherever Books Are Sold

Get all The Clique you crave online!

Visit Lisi Harrison at

www.lisiharrison.com

and

Win prizes, get downloads,
and chat with other Clique fans at

www.jointheclique.com

Welcome to Poppy.

A poppy is a beautiful blooming red flower
(like the one on the spine of this book). It is also
the name of the new home of your favorite series.

Poppy takes the real world and makes it
a little funnier, a little more fabulous.

Poppy novels are wild, witty, and inspiring.
They were written just for you.

So sit back, get comfy, and pick a Poppy.

poppy

www.pickapoppy.com